TABLOIDOLOGY

Chris McMahen

ORCA BOOK PUBLISHERS

Library and Archives Canada Cataloguing in Publication

McMahen, Chris

Tabloidology / written by Chris McMahen.

ISBN 978-1-55469-009-1

I. Title.

PS8575.M24T32 2009   jC813'.54   C2008-907662-1

First published in the United States, 2009
Library of Congress Control Number: 2008942004

Summary: Bizarre things happen when a wild girl and a serious boy are forced to
work on their school's newspaper together.

Orca Book Publishers gratefully acknowledges the support for its publishing programs
provided by the following agencies: the Government of Canada through the Book
Publishing Industry Development Program and the Canada Council for the Arts, and
the Province of British Columbia through the BC Arts Council
and the Book Publishing Tax Credit.

Design by Teresa Bubela
Cover artwork by Monika Melnychuk
Author photo by Ben McMahen

ORCA BOOK PUBLISHERS   ORCA BOOK PUBLISHERS
PO Box 5626, STN. B   PO Box 468
VICTORIA, BC CANADA   CUSTER, WA USA
V8R 6S4   98240-0468

www.orcabook.com
Printed and bound in Canada.
Printed on 100% PCW recycled paper.
12 11 10 09 • 4 3 2 1

For Heather

ONE

On Wednesday night at 8:58 PM, Martin Wettmore rubbed his eyes. He'd been staring at his computer screen for the past five and a half hours. Beside Martin's keyboard was a stack of thirty pages, each covered in his neat, precise handwriting. On a bulletin board above his desk were fifteen photographs lined up in three rows of five.

The door to his room flew open. Martin's older brother Razor barged in, lugging his electric guitar and amp.

"You're not practicing now, I hope," Martin said. "I have work to do."

Razor plugged in his guitar and amp, turned a few dials and smacked the guitar strings with his thumb. A puff of smoke rose from the amp as the windows rattled and the floor vibrated.

"YEAH! SWEET!" Razor shouted, thrashing at his guitar, twisting and bending with each whack of the strings.

Martin tore off two pieces of paper from his notepad, scrunched them into tiny balls and stuffed them in his ears. He rubbed his eyes once more and then looked down at the sheets of paper on his desk.

Even through his makeshift earplugs, Martin could hear his mother open the door and scream, "TURN THAT RACKET OFF! YOU KNOW YOU'RE NOT SUPPOSED TO PLAY THAT THING AFTER EIGHT O'CLOCK!" Martin looked up to see his mother, in housecoat and slippers, yank the plug from the wall.

"Hey!" Razor said. "I'm working on a new tune for our album!"

"I don't care. It's too loud!" Martin's mother said.

"When our band gets our big record deal, you won't be pulling the plug," Razor said.

"Well, I don't want your racket ruining my batch of pickles!" his mother said. "I've told you how sensitive my pickles are. A loud noise might ruin the whole batch."

"What's the big deal?" Razor said.

"I'll tell you what the big deal is. The North Valley Agricultural Exhibition Pickle Competition, that's what! I've got first place in the bag as long as that racket from your guitar doesn't ruin everything."

Martin could still hear way too much. He jammed the balls of paper further into his ears.

His mother slammed the door and thumped down the stairs. But just as Martin hunkered down in front of his computer again, he heard his sister Sissy shouting from the bottom of the stairs. "Martin! One of the dogs just pooped in the hall. It's your turn to clean it up!"

"If your dog pooped in the hall, shouldn't you clean it up?" Martin yelled back.

"Don't argue with me, Martin. I don't have time. I'm right in the middle of whitening Teacup's teeth," Sissy said.

"But I'm right in the middle of working on my—"

"Do what your sister says, Martin!" his mother yelled. "No dillydallying around. Clean it up now!"

Martin wrote on his pad of sticky notes *Buy proper earplugs.* Then he grabbed a couple of crumpled pieces of paper from his garbage can, trudged into the hall and scooped the poop. He went to the bathroom, flushed everything down and turned on the taps in the sink to wash his hands. The pipes made a hollow sucking sound. No water came out of the faucet. "Not again," he said. It was the twenty-seventh time the water had cut out since they'd moved into the house last year. Martin washed his hands with a damp sani-towel from a box his mother kept in the medicine cabinet for times like this.

At 9:07 PM, Martin got back to his desk. Razor was talking on his cell phone to his latest girlfriend. He called her Blade. Martin tried to stuff the paper balls even deeper into his ears and hunched over a sheet of paper. He ran his fingers slowly over each sentence, mouthing the words as he read. Every so often, he'd stop and hiss through his teeth, "No! No! No! That's not good enough!" He grabbed a red pen from the pottery pencil-holder he'd made in grade two, and scribbled, crossed out, corrected and then scribbled, crossed out and corrected some more. Turning the paper over, he began to work on the next page when a large drop of water landed *splat* in the middle of the paper. It was soon followed by another and another.

Martin looked up and saw a huge stain in the ceiling above his desk. The last time it rained, the water had dripped on his bed. Razor and his friends must have made a hole in the roof when they were teeing golf balls off the roof last week. Martin grabbed the end of his desk and shoved it out of the drip's way.

"Terrence, are you moving the furniture around again?" Martin's mother said from out in the hall. Terrence was Razor's real name. His mother was the only person who called him Terrence.

Martin opened the bedroom door and said, "There's another leak in the roof, Mom. I had to move my desk."

"Another leak?" his mother said. "What are you boys doing in that room? Firing your pellet guns through the ceiling or something?"

At 9:13 PM, Martin returned to his computer and began to type rapidly using his thumbs and index fingers. He stopped and looked back over the red-splotched paper. "NO! That's not good enough! Not good enough!" With both hands, he grabbed the paper, tore it four times, crumpled the scraps into a ball and threw it against the wall.

"Come on, Martin. You can do better than this." As he banged his forehead with his fists, his desk began to vibrate. Everything in the room began to shake. The dirty cups and glasses on the dresser rattled, Razor's belt buckles on the floor of the closet chittered and chattered. Martin's computer mouse skittered toward the edge of the mouse pad. With one hand, he grabbed his keyboard and with the other he steadied his monitor. It was the 9:18 express train, rumbling past on the tracks behind the house.

At 9:27 PM, Martin leaned on his elbows, his nose almost touching the computer screen. He read, re-read and re-re-read what he'd typed until he sniffed burning plastic. His old monitor was overheating again. He switched it off, fanned the back with a piece of cardboard, waited ten minutes and turned it back on.

At 9:44 PM, Martin's eyes were back on the computer screen, and he was gritting his teeth until his jaw hurt. "That's just not right. It's got to be better!" he said, bumping his fore-head against the screen three times.

At 9:45 PM, Sissy's five dogs started to bark. Every night at this time, they barked for about fifteen minutes and then suddenly stopped. No one knew why.

Martin took another look at the words he'd typed and slammed his fist on the desk. He leaped up, kicked back his chair and began pacing back and forth across the tiny room, clutching the sides of his head. "Think. Think. Think, Martin! You've got to get it right. It's got to be perfect!"

☆ ☆ ☆

On Wednesday night at 8:58 PM, Trixi Wilder was sprawled across the plush pink carpet next to her pink canopy bed.

The TV in the corner cabinet was off. Her cell phone was turned off and so were her satellite radio, CD, DVD and Mp3 players. Trixi wanted no distractions, for she was creating the best poem of her life.

"It's perfect!" she whispered as she jumped up and ran across the house to her father's home office. The door was locked. She could hear him talking on the phone, so she skipped down to her mother's office.

Trixi bounced in through the open door. "Hey, Mom! Can you help me finish my poetry assignment? My teacher said I could read my poem into a tape recorder instead of writing it out."

Trixi's mother was hunched over her computer, her eyes fixed to the screen. "Don't you think you should write it out like all the other children, Trixi? I don't like the way you avoid writing. You'll never improve at this rate."

"But I've made up this amazing poem, and I thought it would be so great if you read it into the tape. Sort of like a guest reader. You'd be perfect!"

The phone rang. Mrs. Wilder snapped her fingers and waved Trixi out of the room as she picked up the phone. Trixi waited outside the office door until her mother finished her call.

"I've got that old cassette recorder from the basement, so all you have to do is read my poem into the microphone," Trixi said. "It'll only take a minute."

"Not now, Trixi. I'm getting things in order for our trip to New York. Your father and I are leaving next week," her mother said. "Why don't you get Mrs. Primrose to do it?"

"You're going to New York next week?"

"Yes, I'm sure we mentioned it."

"Can I come this time?"

"That's out of the question. It's a business trip. Go and find Mrs. Primrose. I'm sure she'd be thrilled to read your story."

"It's a poem. And she went off duty half an hour ago. Anyway, you'd read it way better than she ever could."

The phone rang again. "I've got to get this," her mother said, snapping her fingers again and waving Trixi away. "And close the door behind you."

When Trixi heard the click of the lock on her mother's office door, she tore the top sheet off her writing pad. She crumpled her poem into a tight ball and dropped it into the antique Chinese vase by the stairs on her way down to the basement. Once she was inside the laundry room, she locked the door. From a lower cupboard, she took a roll of duct tape and a plastic garbage bag, setting them on the workbench beside the old cassette recorder and her pad of paper. Trixi took a pencil out of her back pocket and began to write.

☆ ☆ ☆

At 10:22 PM, Razor was snoring on his bed while Martin's printer hummed and buzzed, spitting out four sheets of paper. He snatched them up and glanced at a mouse—a live one— running across the top of the printer with a leftover crust from Razor's sandwich. As the last sheet left the printer, everything went dark—the lights, his computer, the printer. His mother must have plugged in the toaster again. Martin fumbled around in his desk drawer for the flashlight.

He carefully laid out the sheets of paper on his desk. Holding a red pen in one hand and the flashlight in the other, Martin examined each sentence and every picture, pausing frequently to scribble, circle or cross out. The moment he'd finished going over all four sheets, the lights, his computer and the printer came back to life.

"Martin, are you still working up there?" his mother called from the bottom of the stairs.

"I'm almost done!"

"I don't care if you're almost done. It's way past your bedtime. Lights out. Now!"

"Got it, Mom," Martin said.

He returned to his computer. There was so much more work to be done.

✩ ✩ ✩

At 10:22 PM, Trixi inserted the batteries in the back of the tape recorder, plugged in the microphone, slid a tape into the player and pressed the Record button. "Testing one, two, three. Testing one, two, three." She rewound the tape and then pressed Play. When she heard her own muffled voice saying, "*Testing one, two, three. Testing one, two, three,*" she said, "This is going to be so good!"

✩ ✩ ✩

At 11:24 PM, Martin was still sitting in front of his computer. He looked up for a second when the smoke detector in the kitchen squealed—another one of Sissy's batches of dog treats left in the oven a little bit too long. For the tenth time that night, he pressed Print, and four pages slid out of the printer.

He spread the papers out on his desk, grabbed his red pen and read each page word by word. Using his grandfather's old magnifying glass, he examined every picture top to bottom and left to right. When he reached the end of the final page, Martin put the cap on his pen, leaned back in his chair, took a deep breath and smiled. "They're going to love it," he whispered. "This time, they're really going to love it."

✩ ✩ ✩

At 11:24 PM, Trixi Wilder pressed the Stop button on the cassette recorder and laughed out loud. "There's no doubt," she said. "This is the best one yet!"

✩ ✩ ✩

The next morning, Martin Wettmore was waiting at the door as the custodian, Mr. Barnes, opened the school. He scooted through the hall to the photocopy room and used a key the principal had given him to unlock the door. Once inside, he punched his four-digit security access code into the photo-copier and got to work.

That same morning, Trixi Wilder arrived at school extra early. Carrying a green garbage bag under one arm, she slipped unseen through the back door, sneaked into the girls' wash-room and got to work.

TWO

It was business as usual at Upland Green School: school buses were on time, parents dropped their children off, students rode their bicycles or walked to school. When the bell rang, everyone headed to class. Teachers talked, students listened—mostly. Long-division questions were answered, the word *because* was misspelled, a game of dodgeball was played in the gym and the librarian read *Buddy Concrackle's Amazing Adventure* to a class. Everyone was doing what they were supposed to be doing at Upland Green School.

All that changed at 9:43 AM when a grade-seven student, Felicity Snodgrass, raised her hand in class and said, "Excuse me, Mrs. Roper. May I go to the washroom?"

"Certainly, Felicity. But hurry back. It's almost recess," her teacher replied.

Felicity ambled down the hallway, taking her time, hoping to dawdle in the washroom until the recess bell. She pushed open the door to the girls' washroom and headed toward the middle stall. As soon as the washroom door swung shut behind her, she froze.

Coming from somewhere in the back of one of the toilets was a gurgling voice:

"I'm so embarrassed that I blushed
For down the toilet I was flushed!
It's really not at all good luck
To be inside a toilet—stuck!
I makes me want to scream and shout
Would someone please come GET ME OUT!"

Felicity bolted from the washroom and ran down the hall screaming, "CALL THE JANITOR! SOMEONE'S FLUSHED THEMSELF DOWN THE TOILET!"

A few minutes later, Brittany Rogers was leaving her class and heading for the same washroom. She pushed the door open, took three steps in and heard,

"The biggest thing I most regret
Stuck inside this small toi-let
Is not that I am cold and wet
But that there is no TV set."

Brittany whirled around, almost tore the washroom door off its hinges and ran back to her classroom.

In the next ten minutes, three more girls ran from the washroom screaming their lungs out. As soon as the recess bell sounded, word spread throughout the school that something very weird and scary was happening in the girls' washroom. Herds of students stampeded down the hall to stand outside the washroom door, too afraid to go in.

"I recognized the voice in the toilet!" Susan McCartney said. "It's that girl, Donna Goodman, who supposedly moved to Calgary. I don't think she really moved. I think she just flushed herself down the toilet!"

"I heard a splashing behind me after it talked!" Jeanette Leblanc said. "I think it was trying to climb out of the toilet!"

"I don't care who it was or what it was!" Clarissa Stoppard gasped. "As long as I go to this school, I'm never going to use the washroom again!"

"I dare you to go in," Trevor Smith said, elbowing his best friend, Blake Turner.

"Are you serious?" Blake said.

"Yeah, I'm serious. What are ya? Chicken?" Trevor said as he began to cluck and flap his arms like chicken wings.

"But it's the girls' washroom!" Blake said.

"So? There aren't any girls in there—just some zombie-alien-toilet-monster thingy. Go ahead! I double-dare ya!"

Trevor kept up the clucking, and he was joined by four other kids, all clucking and flapping their arms. Blake's face was turning a deeper red by the second, until, suddenly, he made a dash through the washroom door.

Everyone in the hall fell silent. Less than five seconds later, the door swung open and Blake ran out screaming, "THERE'S SOMETHING ALIVE IN THERE!" He pushed through the crowd, ran down the hall and out the front door.

☆ ☆ ☆

At the other end of the school was Martin Wettmore. Wearing a dress shirt, a tie and a blue blazer, he sat behind a table, resting his hands on a stack of papers next to a sign: *The latest issue of the* Upland Green Examiner *ON SALE NOW!*

He held up a copy and waved it at anyone who walked past. "Paper! Get your paper! The latest news about our great school. Only twenty-five cents! Read all about the junior soccer team's latest game. Hear all about Mrs. Donnelly's class making a papier-mâché dinosaur. Read next week's weather forecast. You won't want to miss this week's newspaper!"

Unfortunately, no one cared if they did miss this week's newspaper. Martin might as well have been invisible. No one even slowed down on their way to the girls' washroom.

"Oh, come on!" Martin said. "It's only twenty-five cents! And it's full of really interesting stories!" Martin's hand tightened its grip on the copy of the paper. He waved it about and said, "None of you know what you're missing! This is the best edition of the newspaper ever! This time, I even started a *Knock-Knock Joke of the Week* feature. And there's a contest too! Match the teacher with their baby picture. It's interesting! It's really, really interesting!"

Someone did finally stop at Martin's table. It was Trixi Wilder. She snatched a copy of the newspaper off the top of the pile and began to read through it.

"Hey! If you want to read it, you have to pay for it," Martin said. He reached out to grab the paper, but Trixi took two steps back without looking up.

Once she'd read through all four pages of the paper, she slapped it back down on the pile. "Tell me something, Marty. There are four pages of school news in here and not one mention of me! Didn't you hear about the special guest speaker I brought to our class last Monday?"

"I can't include everything that happens around the school in the paper," Martin said. "Ms. Baumgartner only allows me four pages, so I have to choose what I think are the most important stories to put in the paper."

"You consider a story about a papier-mâché dinosaur more important than my guest speaker?" Trixi said. "Come on, Marty. The guy brought his Harley to school and rode it down the hall and right into room thirty-six! Plus, he had a tattoo of a dolphin. You know how everyone loves dolphins!"

"It's not just about what one person finds interesting," Martin said. "I have to choose stories that are important to everyone in the school. That's what journalists do. And anyway, I don't believe he rode his motorcycle down the hall. Ms. Baumgartner would never allow that."

"Okay, then. If the stories you choose to put in your paper are so important, then why doesn't anyone ever buy your newspaper?" Trixi said.

"You think nobody's buying my paper, Trixi? Ha! Just take a look," Martin said. He waved a copy of the newspaper at Brad Wells as he headed past, on his way to the excitement outside the girls' washroom. "Hey, Brad! How about buying a copy of this week's paper? This edition is full of fascinating features! Absolutely fascinating!"

"Yeah, right!" Trixi said. "Really fascinating. Except he left out *the* very most exciting thing that happened in the school this week!"

"Don't listen to her, Brad. Just have a look at what's actually on the front page." Brad hesitated and looked as Martin held up the paper.

"If you're looking for a story about a Harley doing a wheelie down the main hall last Monday, you won't find it," Trixi said. "You also won't see a story about the potbellied pig I brought to school dressed up as Cupid on Valentine's Day. And you won't see a story about the spectacular magic show I did for the kindergarten class."

"There were reasons they weren't reported, Trixi. The pig made a mess, and you set the kindergartners' building blocks on fire!" Martin said. "Come on, Brad. This edition is really good! Please buy a paper!" But Brad shook his head and walked on.

Martin sighed, his arms hanging limply by his sides. After taking a deep breath, he tried again.

"Hey, Trisha! You should buy a paper. Your name's in it! I wrote a story about your class's field trip to the wallpaper factory!" Trisha never even slowed down.

Finally, Martin saw a ray of hope. The principal was heading his way. When Trixi saw Ms. Baumgartner, she made a quick exit, scooting off in the opposite direction.

"Hey, Ms. Baumgartner!" Martin said. "You've got to see the latest edition of the *Upland Green Examiner*. It's the best edition yet! You'll find it very interesting reading."

Ms. Baumgartner took a copy off the top of the pile and handed Martin a quarter. "It doesn't look like you've sold many papers, Martin. How many is it this week?"

"Well, I'm not exactly keeping track," he said.

Ms. Baumgartner quickly flipped through the four pages, nodding and smiling as she read. "Once again, you've maintained your high standards of spelling and grammar, Martin. Very well done," she said.

"Thank you, Ms. Baumgartner. I think this week's edition has some particularly interesting stories, as well. I think you'll find the story about the class trip to the wallpaper factory fascinating."

"Hmm," Ms. Baumgartner replied. "Next week, you might want to print fewer copies, Martin. All these unsold papers just end up in the recycling. And every copy costs the school money."

"But Ms. Baumgartner, I wouldn't want the paper to sell out. I couldn't sleep knowing that some students never got a chance to read about what's happening around their school!"

"We'll talk about this later, Martin," the principal replied. "There's a little problem down at the girls' washroom I have to clear up."

As the principal headed off, Martin waved a copy of his newspaper and shouted, "Get your paper here! *Parking Lot Lines Repainted*. Read all about it in the *Upland Green Examiner*!"

☆ ☆ ☆

The crowd outside the girls' washroom parted when Ms. Baumgartner arrived. "Excuse me, kids," she said. "I have a small plumbing problem to attend to." Inside the washroom, she stopped and listened.

"Stuck in this washroom
I'm so full of gloom.
But although I've been flushed,
I'll never be hushed!"

Ms. Baumgartner walked to the middle cubicle, lifted the lid off the toilet tank and pulled out a garbage bag containing a cassette recorder. She held the dripping bag at arm's length as she left the washroom, walked through the crowd in the hall and headed back to her office.

Moments later, her voice could be heard throughout the school over the PA system. "Could I please have everyone's attention? The problem in the girls' washroom has now been fixed. And could Trixi Wilder please report to the office as soon as possible. Thank you."

A few minutes later, Trixi waltzed through the office door. The school secretary, Mrs. Sledge, said, "I think you know where to sit." Trixi stepped into the principal's office and flopped down on a small, yellow, plastic chair.

Ms. Baumgartner was hunched over her desk, flipping through a file folder stuffed with reports, letters and test results. Across the top of the folder the name *BEATRIX HILDEGARD WILDER* was written in bold, bright red letters.

The principal looked up from her desk and picked the dripping garbage bag containing the cassette recorder up off the floor. "I suppose this was your poetry assignment for Mrs. Green," she said.

"How do you know it was me?" Trixi said.

"Even coming out of a toilet tank, I'd recognize your voice, Trixi."

"Okay, so it was me. But I was just doing what Mrs. Green asked."

"I appreciate your creativity, but I'll let Mrs. Green be the judge of your poetry. My concern is with the location of your poetry reading. You do realize that having a voice coming out of the back of a toilet was a terrifying experience for many of the other students."

"Yeah, but you have to admit," Trixi said, "no one in the school has ever heard poetry coming out of the back of a toilet. It was a first for the school, right?"

"There's no denying it was a first for this school." Ms. Baumgartner shuffled through the papers in the file folder. "In fact, many of the things you've done since arriving at Upland Green School have been 'firsts.' I appreciate your tremendous creativity, but you have to think of the consequences of your actions."

"But most of the kids like what I do. Everyone's still talking about that lunch-hour baseball game we played with the water-filled balloons," Trixi said. "And a bunch of other kids are asking me when I can bring Curly to school again."

"Curly? Who's Curly?" Ms. Baumgartner said.

"The pig I dressed up as Cupid for Valentine's Day."

"Oh, yes. How could I forget?" Ms. Baumgartner said. "The point is, Trixi, as principal, my job is to provide a place where students can learn and teachers can teach without distractions. If someone disrupts the school and interrupts learning, then it is my job to deal with the problem. Do you understand?"

Trixi nodded. She'd heard this speech from Ms. Baumgartner about a million times.

"And furthermore," Ms. Baumgartner said, "I am wondering why an energetic creative student like you refuses to apply herself to schoolwork. There are so many good things you could do in this school with your abilities. Take Martin Wettmore, for example. Look at the wonderful school newspaper he's produced each and every week since he arrived at the school last year."

"Yeah, right. The newspaper no one ever reads," Trixi said.

"That's not the point, Trixi," Ms. Baumgartner said. "Martin puts a great deal of effort into our school newspaper."

"Maybe no one buys it because Martin Wettmore never writes about anything that's interesting. Maybe he can spell *syzygy* with his eyes shut, but when someone like me sets off a Roman candle at sports day, do you think he'll put it in the paper? Forget it! His paper is just plain boring."

"Now, Trixi, don't be so hard on Martin. He works hard at that paper, and his writing abilities are something we should all aspire to."

"I don't know about that," Trixi said. "Don't you think spelling and grammar are just a little overrated?"

Before Ms. Baumgartner could reply, there was a knock on her office door. It was Mrs. Sledge. "Excuse me, Ms. Baumgartner, but the new photocopier technician is here. He was wondering about the problem with the photocopier."

Standing behind Mrs. Sledge was a tall gangly man with a long gray beard and scraggly hair. He was wearing a moth-eaten gray suit much too small for his lanky arms and legs.

"Merlin Pen, at your service!" he said, stepping forward and shaking Ms. Baumgartner's hand.

"Nice to meet you, Mr. Pen," Ms. Baumgartner said. He certainly didn't look anything like the photocopier technicians they'd had before. "Yesterday, someone accidentally dropped their donut into the sheet feeder. Since then, our copier hasn't been working all that well. We're getting a lot of paper jams."

"Ah, I see!" Mr. Pen replied. "It was probably a jam-filled donut! I'll have your beautiful machine back working in harmony in no time."

"Ah...Thank you, Mr. Pen. That sounds...sounds... wonderful," Ms. Baumgartner said.

With a smile and a deep bow, Merlin Pen was off to the photocopy room.

"Now, Trixi," Ms. Baumgartner said, trying to remember where she'd left off. "I can't let the disturbance you created in the washroom go without consequences."

"Are you going to make me write lines again?" Trixi said, rolling her eyes. Two weeks ago, when Ms. Baumgartner was away, the teacher in charge had made Trixi write two hundred times, *I will never ever again put a towel inside the piano right before assembly so that when Mrs. Stokes plays the national anthem the piano doesn't make a sound.*

"No, I'm not going to make you write lines," Ms. Baumgartner said. "Thanks to your poetry reading, the crowd in the hall outside the washroom left all kinds of scuff marks on the floor. After school, I'd like you to help the custodian out by giving the hall an extra scrubbing."

Trixi leaned forward in her chair. "You don't really expect me to scrub the floors, do you, Ms. Baumgartner?" She stood up and stepped across the office to Ms. Baumgartner's desk. Gripping the edge with her fingers, Trixi said, "I've never scrubbed a floor in my entire life! Our housekeeper, Mrs. Primrose, always scrubs the floors. I don't know how it's done!"

"Mr. Barnes will be expecting you outside the door of the custodian's room at three o'clock, Trixi. And tomorrow morning, report to the office to let me know how things went." Ms. Baumgartner rose from her seat, opened her office door and handed the wet garbage bag with the cassette recorder to Trixi. "By the way, Trixi, I've never heard a poem before that rhymes *regret* with *toilet*. Very clever."

THREE

The next morning, Trixi knocked on Ms. Baumgartner's office door. There was no reply, so she knocked again. "Hello? Ms. Baumgartner? It's me, Trixi. Trixi Wilder. Remember? I was supposed to report to you this morning?" There was still no reply, so she gave the door a nudge, and it swung open.

Ms. Baumgartner was sitting at her desk, staring at a huge pile of intricate origami creatures. Across the office was Mrs. Sledge, standing ankle-deep in dozens and dozens of cranes, elephants, frogs, birds, horses, dogs and cats, all neatly folded out of plain white paper.

"Wow, Ms. Baumgartner," Trixi said. "The two of you must really be into origami. I particularly like the elephant, although you might want to make it out of more colorful paper next time."

Ms. Baumgartner looked at Trixi and shook her head. "The photocopier."

"The photocopier?" Trixi replied.

"Yes, the photocopier," Ms. Baumgartner said. "The photo-copier did this."

"You mean, the photocopier folded all these animals?"

Ms. Baumgartner just nodded.

"That's incredible!" Trixi said. "That's even more amazing than a toilet reading poetry!"

"Yes, Trixi. It certainly is amazing—but not in a good way," Ms. Baumgartner said. She picked up a frog and began to flatten out the paper. "Every time a teacher tries to photocopy a worksheet or a test, the copies come out as origami animals. Mr. Wainwright's math test was turned into thirty frogs. Mrs. Donaldson's newsletter came out as twenty-eight paper horses."

"Is there some special origami setting on the machine or something?" Trixi said.

"Unfortunately not. I checked the user's manual. It copies double-sided booklets with hole punches and staples, but I didn't see any mention of origami animals," Ms. Baumgartner said.

"That's amazing."

"It certainly is. But we'll have to get Mr. Pen in here to fix the problem."

Ms. Baumgartner picked up the phone, but before dialing, she looked up at Trixi and said, "By the way, I think you have a hidden talent."

"I do?" Trixi said.

"Yes, Trixi, you do. The hall looked spectacular this morning. Here," she said, picking up a piece of paper off her desk, "have a giraffe."

✩ ✩ ✩

The following Thursday, Martin was back behind his table in the hall attempting to sell the latest edition of the *Upland Green Examiner*.

"Get your paper here!" Martin called. "Read all about it! The latest in school news!"

As usual, the first person to stop by was Trixi Wilder. She snatched up a copy from the pile of papers and began reading through it.

"Hey! I keep telling you, you have to pay before you read it," Martin said. This time, he stepped out from behind the table and tried to grab the paper back, but Trixi just kept backing away.

"Nothing!" she said. "Not a word! Not a single mention of the most original poetry assignment in the history of poetry assignments." She stopped and waved the paper in front of Martin. "You don't get it, do you, Marty? People won't buy your paper if your big, splashy, front-page headline is *School Begins Juice-box Recycling Program*."

"It's a very important issue, in case you didn't know," Martin said. "Read the article and find out why!"

"But kids at this school don't really care about the juice-box recycling program." She flipped to the second page. "And they don't really care about *A Day in the Life of a School Bus Driver*."

"I wouldn't be so sure of that. I was quite amazed by Mr. Anderson's account of his day-to-day routine," Martin said. "If you read the whole article, you'll see the great responsibilities and challenges he faces each and every day."

Trixi kept reading, mumbling, "Weather forecast, lunch-hour hockey league scores, new books in the library and a story about a firefighter doing a presentation for Fire Safety Week. And not one word about the photocopier suddenly folding origami?" Trixi said. "One of the most mind-boggling things this school has ever seen, and you don't even mention it in your paper!"

"Photocopier malfunctions are not newsworthy," Martin said.

"Not newsworthy?" Trixi said. "Listen to me, Marty. This week at our school, you had two of the greatest stories any newspaper editor could hope for. Just think of the headlines you could have had: *Photocopier Goes Wild! This Week Origami. Next Week Paper Airplanes?*"

"That's ridiculous," Martin said.

"Or how about *Toilets Reciting Poetry at Upland Green School. What Will They Do Next? Sing Opera? Tap Dance?*"

"That's even more ridiculous. In my newspaper, I just report the facts," Martin said. "My grandfather was a newspaper editor, and he believed in the facts and nothing but the facts. And that's exactly what I've written!"

"Well, no wonder no one buys your paper," Trixi said. "Facts are boring." She breezed by Martin and slapped the paper back on the top of the pile as she headed off down the hall.

"Just because you don't like my paper, doesn't mean everyone else thinks the same way," he said.

Martin sat down behind his table, straightened up the stack of unsold papers and shouted, "Get you paper here!

Read all about Upland Green's new outside drinking fountain. Read all about it!" But as long as Martin sat there—through recess, lunch hour and for half an hour after school—not one single copy of the *Upland Green Examiner* was sold.

After school, as Martin packed up his unsold newspapers, Ms. Baumgartner came over to buy a copy.

"How did newspaper sales go today, Martin?"

"Oh, about average," he replied.

"Still a lot of unsold papers, Martin," Ms. Baumgartner said, flipping through the stack of newspapers. Martin just shrugged as the principal began to read the paper. "Your stories are all very factual, and as usual your spelling and grammar are impeccable. But have you considered changing the sorts of things you report on in the newspaper? Perhaps you should think about writing articles our students would find a little more…a little more…entertaining."

Martin leaped to his feet, clutching a copy of the newspaper against his chest. "Ms. Baumgartner, as I told you when I took this job, the purpose of a newspaper is to inform its readers with facts. Entertainment has no place in a school newspaper. If the students of this school want entertainment, let them read comic books!"

Ms. Baumgartner sighed, left her quarter on the table and headed back to her office.

FOUR

Trixi didn't walk to school the next morning. Her parents brought her. They drove from their home to school in silence. They marched across the parking lot in silence. They stomped up the front walkway to the school in silence, passing Ms. Baumgartner talking to Merlin Pen.

"So, you're sure it's fixed," Ms. Baumgartner said.

"You bet! It's all fixed and ready to go," Merlin Pen said with a grin that showed off three missing teeth.

"No more origami animals?" Ms. Baumgartner asked.

"No more origami animals," Merlin Pen replied.

"What possibly could have happened to make the photocopier fold origami animals?" Ms. Baumgartner said. "I find it mind-boggling that it would do such a thing."

"These machines aren't simply a collection of nuts and bolts, Ms. Baumgartner. Sometimes they can do things that are downright amazing." Merlin Pen smiled again, made a deep bow and shuffled off down the sidewalk.

Seconds after Merlin Pen was gone, Trixi's parents barged through the front door with Trixi in tow and headed straight for Ms. Baumgartner's office. The principal followed, closing the door behind her.

"Please, have a seat," Ms. Baumgartner said, but the Wilders remained standing.

"I don't know what kind of school you run here, Ms. Gaumbartner," Mrs. Wilder said, "but my husband and I were getting ready for a business trip to New York, and do you know what Trixi did to my dear little white toy poodle, Mitzi? She dyed her hair purple! Did you hear what I said, Ms. Gaumbartner? Purple!"

The principal nodded and said, "Yes, purple. And it's Baumgartner."

"She said it was some sort of art project. I don't know what strange ideas your teachers have about art, but dying my sweet Mitzi's hair purple is not my idea of fine art!"

"Yes, absolutely," Ms. Baumgartner said. She glanced over at Trixi, whose eyes were fixed on the tops of her own shoes.

"And this morning, she put glue on the toilet seat! Did you hear what I said, Ms. Gaumbartner? Glue on the toilet seat!"

Ms. Baumgartner nodded. "Yes. Glue on the toilet seat. And it's Baumgartner—with a *B*."

"She said it was some kind of science experiment!

When I was in school, putting glue on toilets seats was certainly not part of our science curriculum!"

"No, I'm sure it wasn't," Ms. Baumgartner replied.

"Our daughter has never behaved like this before! There's only one place she could have learned such behavior. And do you know where that is, Ms. Gaumbartner?"

Ms. Baumgartner didn't answer.

"At your school, Ms. Gaumbartner. Yes! At your school! And as far as I'm concerned, it's all your fault! Right, Reginald?" Trixi's mother glared at her husband.

Mr. Wilder was standing by the door, checking his cell phone for messages. "Oh, uh, absolutely," he mumbled. "Totally the fault of the school."

"And to make matters worse, Trixi's still getting terrible grades. I was appalled to see the trouble she's having in English class. Her spelling is atrocious and her grammar is just awful. Reginald and I were both honor-roll students all through school, so I don't know what you're teaching at this school, but it isn't working. Right, Reginald?"

"Absolutely. Atrocious," he said.

"We do everything we can for our daughter," Mrs. Wilder continued, rapping a scarlet fingernail on Ms. Baumgartner's desk. "We give her piano lessons, swimming lessons, dance classes. We bought her a new computer for her room. Last Easter we sent her skiing with her cousins to Whistler, and last summer she spent seven weeks in Europe with my two sisters! What more can we do? Isn't that right, Reginald?"

"Oh, uh, absolutely," Mr. Wilder mumbled, checking his watch.

"Granted, our careers keep us both busy, but we're doing our part, Ms. Gaumbartner. Unfortunately, you're not doing yours. Right, Reginald?"

"Oh, uh, absolutely."

"We expect accountability. We demand that you do something!" Mrs. Wilder straightened her suit jacket and skirt and marched toward the office door. "We'll be back from our business trip in three weeks. By that time, we expect you to have fixed the problem. Right, Reginald?"

"Oh, uh, absolutely," Mr. Wilder muttered, holding the door open for his wife. Without another word, Mrs. Wilder strode out of the office, followed in silence by Mr. Wilder.

Trixi sat in the small yellow chair and finally looked up at Ms. Baumgartner. She wondered what her principal was going to say. How was she going to *fix the problem*? Would she give her some lines to write? Maybe schoolyard litter duty. Or maybe—worst of all—she'd give her an in-school suspension. Trixi would have to spend every recess and lunch hour sitting in the paper storage room doing math worksheets.

But Ms. Baumgartner didn't say anything. She just took a deep breath and exhaled slowly. Twice more, the principal took slow deep breaths. Finally, she looked as if she was about to say something.

But before one word left Ms. Baumgartner's mouth, the office door swung open and three teachers crowded into the office, each waving fistfuls of paper.

"What is it now?" Ms. Baumgartner said.

"It's the photocopier, again!" shouted Ms. Marshall.

"More origami animals?"

"No! It's much worse than that. Every time we run a test through the photocopier, the copies come out with all the answers already filled in!"

"Are you sure?" Ms. Baumgartner said. "That's unbelievable. How could a photocopier do such a thing?"

"Here, look for yourself!" Ms. Marshall said, handing a pile of papers over to the principal.

Ms. Baumgartner carefully examined a few of the copied tests. A geometry quiz had all the shapes drawn in and all the angles measured. A geography review had all the capital cities of Canada filled in, the main exports of South America written down and even a paragraph on the government of Great Britain written out, complete with a topic sentence.

"I won't even bother checking the user's manual on this problem," Ms. Baumgartner said. "I'm afraid there's nothing we can do until I can get Mr. Pen back to work on the photocopier."

Ms. Baumgartner picked up the phone, but before dialing, she glanced up at Trixi. "We'll have to talk about our meeting with your parents later, Trixi. You can just head down to your classroom and wait for the bell."

Trixi had to smile. She'd been so busy with the dog and the toilet seat last night, she never got around to studying for her geography review test. The next time she saw Mr. Pen, she'd have to thank him.

☆ ☆ ☆

Trixi left the office and headed to her classroom. But halfway down the hall, she noticed something almost as strange as Merlin Pen's photocopier. Water was seeping from under the doors of the library and running into the hallway. Trixi tried to open the doors, but they were locked. The library was only open in the afternoons.

Trixi sprinted back down the hall to the office and ran past Mrs. Sledge, saying, "It's an emergency!" Without knocking, she threw open the principal's office door and shouted, "Ms. Baumgartner! There's water! Lots of it! And it's coming out of the library!"

Ms. Baumgartner was just hanging up the phone, when her head snapped toward Trixi. "There's what coming out of where?"

"Water! H-two-O! Clear liquid that comes out of pipes! And it's coming out of the library!"

"Water? Coming out of the library?" Ms. Baumgartner shot out of her chair and began a wobbly sprint on her high heels down the hall toward the library. By now, the water had spread all the way across the hall and was flowing toward the back doors. Ms. Baumgartner pulled a ring of keys from her pocket and undid the lock. She pushed both doors open, unleashing a wave of water that rushed past them into the hall.

Trixi looked up and saw the sprinkler heads in the ceiling showering water into every corner of the library. Every book, magazine, poster, kit and manual was turning into a pulpy mushy mess. A computer crackled and sparked before dying in a puff of smoke, and a wooden model of the Ugly Duckling bobbed in the story corner.

"Why are the sprinklers on?" Trixi said.

Ms. Baumgartner grabbed the *C* volume of the encyclopedia, held it over her head and began to wade across the library. "There must have been a fire for the sprinklers to come on!"

"If there was a fire, I think it's probably out," Trixi said.

But Ms. Baumgartner had already disappeared out the fire door.

The school was evacuated until the maintenance department could be called in to turn off the sprinklers and the water in the hall could be vacuumed and mopped up. Fortunately, most of the water had run straight down the hall and out the back door, leaving the classrooms dry. Unfortunately, every book, magazine, encyclopedia and computer in the library was waterlogged and useless.

That afternoon, the entire school was called down to the gym for an emergency assembly. Trixi sat obediently in a row with the rest of her classmates. Some were leaning forward and looking her way, while others were pointing. "What?" she whispered. "It wasn't me! I had nothing to do with it!"

Trixi knew she had a reputation for pulling some pretty amazing pranks in the school, but they couldn't blame her for this one. None of her pranks ever caused damage to school property. And they certainly never came close to the chaos caused by the sprinklers in the library. At least, they'd better not blame it on me! she thought.

Trixi noticed Ms. Baumgartner's hair was still wet and tangled from her shower in the library that morning, and she was wearing an old pair of gumboots she'd borrowed from the custodian.

"I just want to reassure everyone in the school that the unfortunate flood in our library was a complete accident. I have heard some nasty rumors circulating about this being a prank, but I can assure you it was caused by faulty sprinkler heads. The bad news is that the contents of the library have been ruined by the water."

There were gasps from various parts of the gym. Hands shot up.

"Excuse me, Ms. Baumgartner," Greg Olson said. "Don't tell me all the Tintin books are gone!"

"I'm afraid so, Greg."

"How about Tom and Liz Austin? And Anne? And the Hardy Boys? And Nancy Drew?" Ella Brown called from the back. "Did they survive?"

"Sadly, no, Ella. Pretty well every single book was damaged beyond repair," Ms. Baumgartner said. "Unfortunately, our insurance will only cover damage to the building. It does not cover the replacement of our books, computers and other materials. This means we're going to have to do some fundraising to restock our library. Not only that, we'll have to take money normally used for other school activities to buy replacement books. To save money, I'm afraid some of our field trips, sports events and other special activities will have to be cut back."

Ms. Baumgartner blinked as a light flashed in front of her. Martin was crouched in the front row, taking a picture for the school newspaper.

FIVE

The next Thursday at recess, Martin sat in the hall at his table with yet another stack of unsold copies of the *Upland Green Examiner*. Once again, the only one to stop at his table was Trixi Wilder.

"So, Marty, with all the excitement of the flood in the library, I bet you wrote one humdinger of an article, giving all the gruesome details. People love reading about disasters. You might actually sell a few copies for a change."

"As with every edition of the *Upland Green Examiner*, I have stuck to the facts—the cold hard facts," he replied.

Trixi snatched up a copy of the paper, but this time Martin didn't even bother asking her to pay.

"*Library Experiences Increase in Water Content.* That's it?" Trixi said. "That's your great headline about the biggest disaster in the history of this school?"

"Before judging the article, I suggest you read it," Martin said, his hands clenched into fists.

Trixi held up the paper and read the article out loud in her best TV news-anchor voice. "*Last Friday, due to some faulty plumbing, a leak occurred in the overhead sprinkler system in the library. The water caused extensive damage to much of the library's collection. The library will be closed until further notice.* That's it?"

"Those are the plain facts. The facts and nothing but the facts," Martin said, his arms now folded tightly across his chest.

Trixi flipped through the rest of the paper. "Mrs. Brown's class going on a field trip to the fire station, Mr. Eastman's class making mobiles out of recycled coat hangers, a day in the life of a school custodian and the weather forecast." Trixi shook her head and slammed the newspaper back on the pile. "Oh, well. At least you didn't leave out anything great I did this week. Although, next week, I'm sure I'll have something spectacular for you to write about. Good luck with sales. I'll let you know if anyone needs to line the bottom of a birdcage."

Moments after Trixi had loped off down the hall, Ms. Baumgartner came by. Without a word to Martin, she snatched up a copy of his newspaper. After a quick read, she shook her head. "Couldn't you make the front-page article just a little more exciting, Martin? You've described the flood as an 'increase in water content.' Don't you think you should jazz your writing up a little?"

"Absolutely not, Ms. Baumgartner!" Martin said, jumping up from his chair. "I reported the flood in a responsible, factual manner. There's no room for sensationalism in my paper!"

"Obviously not," Ms. Baumgartner said. She slapped the paper down on the stack of unsold papers and walked off without a word—not one mention about his fine spelling or his grammar, and not even a hint of her usual smile. Not only that, she didn't even buy a copy. This was not a good sign. Martin could sense something was in the air. He didn't know what, but something at Upland Green School was about to change.

☆ ☆ ☆

That night, Razor's band practiced in the living room until 2:25 AM when the neighbors finally phoned the police.

At 2:55 AM, three fire trucks answered a call, roaring out of the fire station with their sirens wailing.

At 4:42 AM, Sissy's dogs got loose, ran upstairs and jumped up on Martin's bed.

At 4:55 AM, two fire trucks answered another call.

At 5:15 AM, the freight train rumbled past Martin's house, and the engineer blew the whistle three times.

At 5:45 AM, Martin's mother arrived home from working the night shift and tripped over the cat in the front hall.

At 5:55 AM, three fire trucks answered another call.

At 7:30 AM, Martin dragged himself out of bed to take a shower, but there was no water. All he could find for breakfast was a can of sardines, a box of stale crackers and a jar of pickles.

He took the last bruised apple and the rest of the crackers for his lunch and headed for school.

☆ ☆ ☆

Trixi woke up to find a note stuck to the outside of her bedroom door.

I forgot to tell you last night that your father and I had to leave for New York a day earlier than planned. If you behave yourself while we're gone, we'll pick up something special for you at Saks Fifth Avenue.

Be Good,
Mom

☆ ☆ ☆

Right after the first bell rang at school, Ms. Baumgartner's voice was heard over the PA speaker in Martin's classroom. "Mr. Branch? Could I please see Martin Wettmore in my office?"

What with the superintelligent photocopier and a library that turned into a wading pool, yesterday had been a strange day. Now, today was off to a strange start of its own. No one in his class could believe that Martin "Never-Broken-a-Rule-in-His-Life" Wettmore was being called down to the office.

At first Martin figured, in his half-awake state, that he hadn't heard right. But his teacher said, "Martin, you'd better get going. Ms. Baumgartner's asking for you."

"There must be some mistake," Martin said. "Maybe there's another Martin Wettmore in the school. Or maybe there's another kid who looks just like me and she's gotten us mixed up."

"I don't think so," Mr. Branch said. "Let's go, Martin! To the office. Right away."

A moment later, Ms. Baumgartner's voice came over the PA speaker in another class. "Mrs. Green? Could I please see Trixi Wilder in my office?"

This was no surprise to anyone. Trixi's visits to the office were routine.

Unlike Martin, Trixi had a pretty good idea why she was being called down to the office. After her parents' visit to the school yesterday, Ms. Baumgartner never did get around to telling Trixi how she was planning to *fix the problem*. When Trixi walked into Ms. Baumgartner's office and saw Martin Wettmore already sitting in her yellow plastic chair, she wondered, Why is he here? Is he some sort of witness? Is he going to write a first-hand report on my punishment for his boring school newspaper?

As Martin watched Trixi sit in another yellow chair right next to his, he wondered, Why is she here? Is she some sort of witness? Is she going to advise Ms. Baumgartner on the proper punishment to give based upon her vast personal experience?

Instead of sitting behind her desk as usual, Ms. Baumgartner stood in front and leaned against the edge.

"You might be wondering why I've called you both into my office at the same time," she said.

"I think that's a pretty safe thing to say, Ms. Baumgartner," Trixi said. Martin didn't say anything. He just stared at the floor.

"Well, let me tell you. I'll start with you, Martin," Ms. Baumgartner said. "I certainly have to admire the dedication, hard work and tremendous effort you put into the school newspaper each and every week. However..." Ms. Baumgartner paused and folded her arms.

Martin lifted his head when he heard Ms. Baumgartner say *However*. He didn't like the way she said the word.

"However, by my calculations, since taking over the *Upland Green Examiner* you have printed approximately two thousand copies of the newspaper and sold...twenty. That means one thousand nine hundred and eighty unsold newspapers went into the recycling bin. Through sales of the newspaper, you have earned five dollars, while the cost of printing the newspaper has been approximately eight hundred dollars."

Martin jumped to his feet. "I thought you liked the paper! I thought you thought I was doing a good job! I thought you thought I thought—"

"Sit down, Martin," Ms. Baumgartner said. She walked around her desk and sat down. "Here's the situation, Martin. After the flood in the library, the school needs every penny it can get its hands on to buy replacement books. We have to find ways of saving money."

Martin didn't like the sound of this one little bit. This was definitely not shaping up as a "good news" speech.

"There are many people in this school who feel we should shut the school newspaper down," Ms. Baumgartner continued. "I don't want to do that, Martin. I know how much the newspaper means to you. So instead of shutting the newspaper down, I'm giving you another chance. You may continue to write, copy and sell the school newspaper…but under one condition."

Martin gulped and sat up straight in his chair, his hands folded across his lap.

"From now on," Ms. Baumgartner said, "you must sell enough copies of the paper to pay for the costs of photocopying."

"Pay for the costs of photocopying my newspaper?" Martin said.

"Yes. In other words, the newspaper must pay for itself," Ms. Baumgartner said. "If the cost of printing the paper each week is, say, twenty dollars, then you must sell twenty-dollars worth of papers. But if the newspaper can't pay for itself, we will just have to shut it down. I'm afraid we have no choice in the matter. Do you understand, Martin?"

"You're saying that the *Upland Green Examiner* has to pay for itself?" Martin said.

"Yes, Martin. That's exactly what I'm saying."

"Doesn't anyone in this school see how important it is to be informed?" Martin said. "Doesn't anyone see how important it is to know what's going on around the school? The news of the school may not be entertaining, but it's important information! Like my Grandpa Wettmore said—"

"Yes, Martin, we know what your Grandpa Wettmore said. The plain truth is the school can no longer afford to pay for the printing of your paper. You'll just have to sell more copies."

"I will not change the way I write my newspaper just to make it more en...en...entertaining!" he said. "I won't change the news just to sell more papers. The school newspaper is more important than money!" Martin's face had turned a deep red and his hands gripped the sides of the chair tightly enough to turn his knuckles white.

"I'm sorry, Martin," Ms. Baumgartner said. "We simply haven't got the money to print your paper. Either it pays for itself or we'll have to shut it down. It's as simple as that."

Martin slumped in his chair like a rag doll, his eyes staring blankly at the floor.

"Now for you, Trixi," Ms. Baumgartner said, turning in her chair. "You might be wondering what you have to do with all of this."

"Let me take a wild guess," Trixi said, scanning the ceiling. "Could it have something to do with a meeting you had with my parents yesterday?"

"It's not just about that, Trixi," Ms. Baumgartner said. "We are all concerned with your behavior in and out of the classroom. It's not only disruptive to the rest of the school, but it's also affecting your schoolwork."

"Oh, brother," Trixi said, sliding down in her chair. "Here it comes."

"However," the principal continued, "we all recognize that you have some very special talents. Although your 'activities' cause disruptions in our school, they do show a great deal of creativity and careful planning. The problem, Trixi, is that your talents are being wasted. They're being used for the wrong purposes."

"Uh, Ms. Baumgartner? Does Martin have to hear all this?" Trixi said.

"Actually, he does. Here's the reason why I have you both here," Ms. Baumgartner said. "We have you, Martin—an excellent writer with a newspaper that isn't selling. Then we have you, Trixi—someone who doesn't like to write, but is full of incredibly creative ideas."

Martin and Trixi glanced at one another. Neither of them liked where Ms. Baumgartner's lecture was heading.

"I'm suggesting that the two of you work together on the school newspaper. Martin's attention to the facts and his outstanding spelling and grammar will be combined with Trixi's creativity and imagination. Together, the two of you will produce a school newspaper that students will be eager to read and buy."

"You're not serious, are you?" Trixi said, rising out of her seat. "This is just some sort of sick joke, right?"

"Sit down, Trixi. This is no joke. I am completely serious."

"But I hate writing! You know I'm no good at it. The paper will be full of bad spelling and wrong words in the wrong places. Think how bad it'll make the school look!"

"That's why you and Martin are the perfect team," Ms. Baumgartner said. "You've got the ideas, and he can help you with the writing."

"She'll ruin my newspaper!" Martin said, jabbing a finger in Trixi's direction. "She'll destroy it! She does that to everything!"

"The two of you must learn to work together," Ms. Baumgartner said. "That's all there is to it."

"Work together!" Martin howled. "I can't work with... with...her! I hate her! And she hates me!"

"Now, Martin, *hate* is a very strong word," Ms. Baumgartner said.

"Not in this case," Trixi said. "In fact, I'd say it's probably not strong enough!"

"But I didn't think you even knew each other. You're in different classes, and you don't have the same friends. How can you dislike someone you barely know? I just assumed—"

"Well, you assumed wrong!" Trixi jumped out of her seat again.

Ms. Baumgartner cleared her throat and pointed at the chair. Trixi sat down.

"The two of you will just have to work things out," Ms. Baumgartner said. "Remember our school motto: Cooperation, Kindness and Caring."

"I know our school motto," Trixi said, "and if you must know, only the teachers believe in it. None of the kids do."

Ms. Baumgartner's eyes widened as she tilted her head back. "Do you believe in our school motto, Martin?"

"Yes, except when it comes to her," Martin said, throwing a quick glance at Trixi. "We've hated each other since my first day at this school."

"Yeah," Trixi said. "We've never liked each other. Ever."

"She's right, Ms. Baumgartner," Martin said, looking the principal in the eye. "The first day I was here, she poured chocolate milk down the back of my shirt."

"He's right," Trixi said. "My friends and I thought it was a good way to welcome him to the school."

"That's right!" Martin said, nodding rapidly. "And she and her friends threw snowballs at me on my way home and hit me in the eye!"

"Martin's right. We figured he deserved it because he's the geekiest kid in the entire school."

"Precisely!" Martin said, nodding his head even faster. "And Trixi's got to be the most obnoxious person I've ever met!"

"Absolutely!" Trixi replied. "And let's not forget to mention Martin's bad breath. It's so bad, it could knock a buzzard off a manure spreader!"

"She's right! And she's got the personality of a bag of rusty nails!"

"I couldn't agree with you more!" Trixi grinned.

"So you can see, Ms. Baumgartner, it would be impossible for the two of us to work together on the newspaper," Martin said.

"Martin's right. We'd never be able to agree on anything! And besides," Trixi said, "you can't *force* us to work together."

"You're absolutely right, Trixi," the principal said. "I can't force you to work on the paper, so I'll give you two choices."

"Two choices? Okay. What are they?"

"Choice number one: you can work together and make the school newspaper a success," Ms. Baumgartner said.

"Yeah, yeah, sure thing," Trixi said. "What's choice number two?"

"Choice number two: we shut the newspaper down, and you, Trixi, can spend the next ten Saturdays washing school buses. I'm sorry it's come to this, Trixi, but things have reached a point where your antics just can't go on any longer. You've got to stay out of trouble and apply yourself to your school-work. That's the only way your skills will improve. I'm giving you an opportunity to do all that with the school newspaper. So, what'll it be?"

Trixi sighed. "Is there a choice number three?"

✧ ✧ ✧

As Martin left the principal's office, he felt like he'd been kicked in the stomach by a horse, whacked in the shins by a kangaroo and punched in the nose by a gorilla. The *Upland Green Examiner* wasn't really the *school's* newspaper. It was *his* news-paper. Every dotted *i* and crossed *t* was his doing. No one else in the school was good enough to work on *his* paper, especially not Trixi Wilder!

Martin's only hope was that Trixi would rather wash school buses than work on the newspaper. But knowing Trixi, that wasn't very likely. As Martin headed to class, he was madly trying to figure out a way to outsmart Trixi and prevent her from completely ruining his newspaper.

☆ ☆ ☆

As Trixi walked home, she thought about what had happened in Ms. Baumgartner's office. She wasn't too crazy about the choices Ms. Baumgartner had given her: wasting her lunch hours writing some dumb school newspaper with Martin Wettmore or getting up early Saturday mornings to wash school buses.

Trixi halted on the sidewalk in front of her house and stood tapping the side of her head with a finger. Washing school buses or working on the school newspaper? Which one offered more possibilities? She could paint the school buses different colors or install whoopee cushions on all the seats. What about the newspaper? What sort of fun could she possibly have with a school newspaper? How much fun could she have writing about lunch-hour floor-hockey games or field trips to a wallpaper factory or...

And then, Trixi's mouth stretched into the biggest smile her face had ever made.

Yes! She would work on the newspaper. Forget about her other pranks. Talking toilets, Harleys in the hallway and purple-haired dogs were small potatoes compared to what she could do with the school newspaper! Trixi's mind was spinning with possibilities. This newspaper was a chance to have way more fun than the rest of her pranks combined. Ms. Baumgartner had no idea what she was getting herself into.

SIX

Ms. Baumgartner set out a few rules for running the newspaper. Trixi and Martin were to have a weekly newspaper meeting every Monday at noon in the computer lab. At this meeting, they would plan out the stories to be written for that week's edition of the newspaper.

At their first meeting, Martin arrived five minutes early and pulled a chair up to an empty table at the back of the room. He drummed his fingers on the table, glancing at the clock every few seconds. In his dreams, Trixi wouldn't show up.

The clock read 11:59. No sign of Trixi. Maybe she was too busy switching the signs on the boys' and girls' change-room doors. Or maybe she was in the middle of turning a garter snake loose in the staff room. Or maybe she'd decided to wash school buses instead of work on the paper. Martin remained hopeful.

He pulled some sheets of paper out of his backpack, straightened the paper clip holding them together and laid them down carefully with the bottom of the papers lined up perfectly with the edge of the table.

Martin glanced at the clock. 12:01. Still no Trixi. Maybe she was turning all the class pets loose or dropping water-filled balloons off the roof or taking the air out of all the volley-balls in the gym. Why would a troublemaker like Trixi want to work with him on the school newspaper? What was Ms. Baumgartner thinking?

At 12:02, the door swung open and there stood Trixi, her cheeks bulging like a squirrel who'd just won an acorn lottery. In one hand was a half-eaten submarine sandwich and in the other a can of Zappo cola.

Martin jumped out of his chair and said, "Ms. Hart's number one rule is no food or drink in the computer lab. If she sees you, you'll be in big trouble!" Trixi shrugged, flopped into a chair and slammed her can of cola down on the table.

The two of them stared across the table at each other. Trixi chewed on her gigantic sandwich, while Martin nibbled on his thumbnail. Usually Trixi got in the first word, along with the second word and the next five thousand words. But with her mouth stuffed full of submarine sandwich, Martin went on the attack—the future of his newspaper was at stake. He reached across the table and carefully laid down the pile of neatly stacked papers in front of Trixi.

"Here is the next edition of the *Examiner*," he said, wiping beads of sweat off his forehead with his sleeve. "All the stories are written, all the pictures are in place and, as usual, there are no spelling or grammatical errors."

Trixi kept chewing as she glanced at the papers in front of her. A sound came from somewhere deep in her throat. Martin couldn't tell exactly what the sound meant. Either she was trying to say something or she was choking on her sandwich.

He reached across the table and tapped the front page with his finger. "The front-page story, *Trees Trimmed at Front of School*, is about the trimming of the trees at the front of the school." His voice was louder than it had to be, and the words flew out faster than he'd ever spoken in his life.

"I interviewed the two workers cutting the tree branches and got a detailed, step-by-step description of the science of tree pruning. Everyone should find this article fascinating!"

Trixi gulped and made an awful face as she tried to swallow a wad of sandwich far too big for her throat. Martin just kept talking, flipping the page and tapping his finger on the head-line across the top of page two.

"*Obedient Dogs at Upland Green School.* It's about the dog obedience class that's held in our gym on Tuesday nights. I'm particularly proud of the photograph I took of Terry Springate's dog Sparky rolling over on command."

Trixi kept trying to swallow, but the wad of sandwich was stuck. She grabbed her can of cola and tipped it back to her mouth.

"And I interviewed our new school crossing guard, Mr. Dobson. You wouldn't believe the amazing stuff I found out."

Trixi swallowed a few more times. The cola was slowly turning the wad of sandwich in her throat into mush.

"And then there's the weekly weather forecast: cloudy with sunny breaks and a chance of showers. Very unusual for this time of year," he said.

Martin straightened the papers, once more carefully aligning the bottom of the pages with the edge of the table in front of Trixi. He gave the stack of papers three gentle pats with the palm of his hand and said, "It may sound like I'm bragging, but the truth is, this is the best edition yet. Every article is based on solid facts."

Trixi swallowed, took a few deep breaths and a couple more swigs of cola, but she still couldn't speak.

Martin knew he didn't have much time before Trixi would unleash her own barrage of words, so he stood up and pointed across the table at her. "We're supposed to be working together on the newspaper, so to keep Ms. Baumgartner happy, here's your part. All you have to do is take the paper to the office, get a security code number for the photocopier from Ms. Baumgartner, print one hundred copies and sell them in the front hall tomorrow at recess and lunchtime. That's it. Nothing more. You don't have to do anything else."

Martin turned, ran across the computer lab and out the door, slamming it for effect. Once he was outside the room, he collapsed against the wall and exhaled like he was blowing up some gigantic imaginary balloon.

He'd done it! He'd shown Trixi who was the boss! He'd shown her that Martin Wettmore was the one in charge. Martin undid the top button of his shirt, hitched up his pants and smiled. Nothing was going to stop the *Upland Green*

Examiner from being Martin Wettmore's newspaper. Not even Trixi Wilder.

☆ ☆ ☆

By the time Trixi could finally talk, Martin was long gone. She picked up the paper and flipped through the pages. "Who would ever be interested in this garbage?" she shouted to the empty room. "And no one orders me around! What does he think I am? His personal secretary?" Trixi slammed the table with her fist. The can of Zappo cola jumped, wobbled and tipped over. As a dark brown, gooey liquid oozed across the tabletop, the computer-room door swung open. Trixi looked up to see Ms. Hart, the computer teacher. Her eyes went back and forth between Trixi and the puddle of Zappo cola.

"What is the meaning of—?"

"Ms. Hart! Did you see Martin Wettmore running out of here? He spilled his soft drink all over the table and ran out without cleaning it up!"

Ms. Hart narrowed her eyes and folded her arms, giving Trixi a look she'd seen from adults way too often. Trixi knew it was time for some serious damage control. The Zappo cola was already starting to turn the tabletop an odd color, so she grabbed the closest thing she could find and started mopping up the pool of sticky liquid.

When all the spilled drink was cleaned up, she tossed the lump of pulpy paper into the garbage. "Martin's school newspaper has never been so useful," she said.

☆ ☆ ☆

The next day, an historic event took place at Upland Green School. Trixi Wilder visited the principal's office and was not in trouble. She breezed into the office before school with a few crisp clean pieces of paper under her arm.

"Ms. Baumgartner! I've got the first edition of the all-new school newspaper ready to copy."

The principal smiled. It was a smile of relief. "Wonderful! Great! I was worried that…I mean, I knew you and Martin could work well together. I can't wait to read it!"

Trixi wagged her finger and said, "Patience, patience, Ms. Baumgartner. You'll have to buy a copy when the paper goes on sale just like everyone else."

Trixi grinned. Ms. Baumgartner smiled back, but it was a nervous smile.

"But no one's going to read it," Trixi said, "unless I can make some copies. And to make copies of it, I'll need my own security code number for the photocopier."

"Right!" Ms. Baumgartner said. "You're in luck. Mr. Pen happens to be here right now."

"More trouble with the photocopier?" Trixi said.

"Yes. It's very strange. Very strange, indeed. This morning, for some reason, all of our copies came out of the machine printed in Japanese. Imagine that!" Ms. Baumgartner said, as she led Trixi down the hall to the photocopy room. "I'm sure he's got it fixed by now. He should be able to program in a new security code for you right away."

Ms. Baumgartner opened the door to the photocopy room. "Good heavens, Mr. Pen! What are you doing?" she said. The floor of the photocopy room was covered in dozens and dozens of bolts, screws, wires, pieces of plastic, cables, rollers, spools, belts and twisted bits of metal. Standing in the middle of it all was Merlin Pen, scratching his head.

"Don't you worry, Ms. Baumgartner!" he said with a smile. "I have the situation completely under control. I'll have your machine back together in a jiffy."

"Was it really necessary to take the photocopier apart completely?" Ms. Baumgartner said.

"A photocopier that translates everything into Japanese is a serious problem, ma'am. I'm determined to get to the bottom of this."

Ms. Baumgartner rubbed her forehead with the tips of her fingers and shook her head slowly. "How long do you expect it to take before the machine will be in working order?"

"I'll have everything back together in a jiffy. Don't you worry. We'll have your photocopier cranking out copies in no time flat! And if everything goes right, they'll be in English."

Ms. Baumgartner shook her head and said, "It'll take some magic to get that old photocopier working normally." As she turned to leave, she added, "After you've gotten the machine working, please give Trixi a security code number for the photocopier. And while you're at it, you can erase Martin Wettmore's code. Trixi will be photocopying the school newspaper from now on."

"That I'll do in two shakes!" Merlin Pen said with a twinkle in his eye.

Ms. Baumgartner left Trixi to watch Merlin Pen work on the photocopier.

"Now, there you go, Gwennie," he said, giving the side of the photocopier a loving pat with his hand. "Nice and easy, there. Just hold on. This may be a little painful, but when I'm done, you'll feel fit as a fiddle. Just take 'er easy now. Don't move while I'm putting this part in."

"Are you talking to the photocopier?" Trixi said.

"Why, of course I am," Merlin Pen said. "Gwennie's a delicate machine, so she needs reassurance while she's being fixed."

"Do you have names for all of your photocopiers?"

"Of course I do! There's Matilda, Viviane, Avalon, Chelinda and, of course, good old Blancheflour. They deserve names just like people and pets do. Say, while you're standing there, how about passing me that bit of wire over there by your right foot."

While Merlin Pen talked soothingly to the photocopier, Trixi handed him the pieces one by one. Very gently, he put the pieces back in place until, miraculously, everything seemed to be in order and the photocopier purred peacefully.

Turning to Trixi, he said, "Now, you might think this machine is just a bunch of nuts and bolts and wires and screws, but let me tell you something." He paused and looked toward the door as if making sure no one else was listening. Scribbling a number on Trixi's hand with a felt pen, he whispered,

"Here is your secret security code number. If you treat Gwennie with some kindness and tenderness and respect, you'll be amazed at the wonderful things she can do for you. In fact, she might change your life." Merlin snatched his tools off the floor and disappeared out the door.

Trixi looked down at the number written on her hand and shrugged. "Okay, Gwennie. Whatever it is you do, it's time to work some magic."

She punched in her four-digit security code number and waited. The photocopier hummed, clicked and rattled as it usually did while it churned out copies of the latest edition of the Upland Green school newspaper. Everything looked perfectly normal: no origami frogs, no Japanese writing. The photocopier was once again acting like a photocopier. Merlin Pen's words were forgotten as Trixi scooped up her papers and headed out the door. She had other things on her mind— like selling an edition of the school newspaper no one would ever forget.

SEVEN

It was a big day for Martin when the next edition of his newspaper went on sale. He headed down the hall at recess just to make sure Trixi was following his orders. He wanted to be sure she'd printed enough copies. He wanted to double-check that she'd set up the table in the right place and had an empty can with a slot cut in the top for the money. He wanted to see with his own eyes that she was doing everything just right.

The moment he turned the corner and looked down the hall, Martin knew something was wrong. Surrounding the table where Trixi was selling the newspaper was a mob of kids. He hadn't witnessed a scene like this since his mother dragged him down to the Bargain Blowout at Bloom's Department Store to buy socks. There was pushing and shoving, and there were shouts of, "Hey! Get outta my way!" and "Quit butting in line!" and "I was here first!" There was even a bleeding nose and a couple of bruised shins.

Above all this mayhem, Martin could hear Ms. Baumgartner's voice louder than all the rest. "Everybody calm down! Get in a nice straight line. Keep your hands and feet to yourselves."

Out of the tangle of arms, legs and heads, a few kids staggered out of the crowd, clutching crumpled bunches of papers and gasping, "I got one! I got one!"

David Goldman, a kid who normally only talked to Martin when he had him in a headlock, walked by and slapped him on the back. "Way to go, Witless! You finally wrote some good stuff! This paper's great!"

"Oh...really?" Martin said. "Do you really mean that?"

"Yeah!" David said. "That story about the maple trees is so great!"

"Really?" Martin said. "You really liked it?"

"Oh, yeah! The best twenty-five cents I ever spent in my entire life!"

Martin was shocked and delighted.

He was even more shocked when Mercedes Milano ran past him waving a copy of the newspaper, headed for the front door of the school.

"Hey, Mercedes! What are you doing?" Martin called.

"The weather forecast! My mom's apple orchard! I've got to let her know about the weather forecast!"

Wow. Martin had never seen anyone so worked up about a weather forecast. Especially his weather forecast. Still, it was nice to see people paying attention to his scientifically determined predictions. He was finally getting the attention he deserved.

Above the rumble of the crowd, Phil Shipley was shouting something at Martin. This was the same Phil Shipley who had dropped the class's pet mouse down the back of Martin's pants in the change room after gym class last week. "Hey! I gotta talk to you. That sounds like some dog obedience class! I'm thinking of enrolling my Chihuahua. Do you think she'd be too short?"

"Ah…well…er…I don't know. You'll have to ask the teacher, I guess."

This was great! Finally, everyone at Upland Green School recognized how great their school newspaper really was! Martin basked in this, his finest hour.

Or maybe his finest minute.

Everything changed very quickly. Too quickly. Ms. Baumgartner fought her way out of the crowd and said, "Martin! In my office. Now!"

Martin had never heard Ms. Baumgartner speak like this before. He didn't like the way she barked out his name, or the way she spat out the word *office*. He especially didn't like the way she added *Now!* at the end. Martin's legs began to shake, and he felt an almost irresistible urge to throw up.

He hustled down to Ms. Baumgartner's office and sat obediently in one of the yellow plastic chairs. "What…what… what is it, Ms. Baumgartner?" he croaked.

The principal leaned into the office and said, "You and your partner have some explaining to do, Martin!" She threw a copy of the newspaper on the floor and rushed back into the hall, shouting, "Everyone calm down. Just calm down!"

How could things change so quickly? How could Martin go from blissful happiness to sheer terror in under sixty seconds? Why was Ms. Baumgartner suddenly so angry?

But then, Martin looked down to the floor and saw the copy of the school newspaper. In huge letters across the front page was the headline:

> *THE REVENJ OF THE MAPEL TREES!!!*
> *Maple Trees Fite Back After Being Trimed!*

Something was terribly wrong here. This wasn't the headline he'd written for the front page! Plus, there were four spelling mistakes! This wasn't *his* paper. It didn't even have the right name! It was called the *Upland Green Gossiper—All the News That's Unfit to Print*!

Martin took all of two seconds to figure out what was going on here.

Trixi.

Trixi Wilder.

This was her doing!

Grabbing the paper, Martin's fingers tightened their grip as he read each word of the butchered article.

> *THE REVENJ OF THE MAPEL TREES!!!*
> *Maple Trees Fite Back After Being Trimed!*
> *by Marton Wetmor*
> Two workers triming the mapel trees at the front of Upland Green School were in for a big surprise last week. As soon as they had

finished cuting off a number of branchs on one tree, the next tree took revenj! With a swift, suden movement, a branch swept down and snached the chainsaw out of the hands of won of the workers. The chainsaw was then tossed across the rode and into the creak. Grounds supervizer, Mr. Mowers, warns all humans to keep a safe distance from thees nastey trees.

More than twenty spelling mistakes in the first article alone. Even his name was spelled wrong! Martin looked at the lower half of the front page and his eyes nearly shot from their sockets when he saw what had become of his article on the dog obedience classes.

DOG OBEDIENSE CLASS GRADUATE DRIVES OUNER TO HOSPITLE AFTER HART ATACK!

by Martan Wettmoar

When Mr. Terry Springate, a substitoot bus driver and local snowplow enthuziast, brought his dog Sparky to dog obediense classes in our school gym, he had no idea his pirky pooch would someday save his life. But sure enough, only two weaks after Sparky, a four-year-old cocker spanial, sucesfully graduated from dog obediense school with straight A's, the owner was saved by his brilliunt dog.

While sitting in his truck in the grosery store parking lot, Mr. Springate sudenly colapsed. Sparky dragged him into the passenger seet and jumped over to the driver's side. Luckily, Mr. Springate had left his truck running and in newtral. Sparky took the geershift in his paw and slipped it into DRIVE. He threw Springate's lunch bucket on the axselerator and managed to stere the truck five blocks to the hospitle parking lot. There, Sparky drove the truck up the furst two steps of the front entrance, where the truck stalled.

"He never would of made it if Sparky hadn't bringed him in," said Dr. Grant Willow. "He's an amayzing dog!"

But Constuble Bruce Jefferies wasn't quite so impresed. "That dog broak every law in the book. For starters, he's under age for a driver's lisense, he ran three stop signs, and our raydar clocked him going seventy in a fifty zone. On top of that, the front steps of the hospitle is a NO PARKING zone. If he had a driver's lisense, I'd suspend it!" the angry police officer went on to say.

If your intrested in teaching your dog how to drive, be sure to contact Ms. Julia Pimlott, dog obediense instructer.

Martin's story had been hacked, thrashed and mutilated. Even the picture of Sparky had been changed. There was the dog with his paws on the steering wheel of a truck!

Martin wasn't sure exactly how he felt. It was more than disappointment, dismay, anger or horror. It was a feeling so strong Martin didn't even have a word for it. And that was saying something.

Could page two be any worse? After all, it was the weather forecast. What could she possibly do to his weather forecast?

THIS WEEK'S WEATHER FOURCAST
by Martn Wettmorr

Acording to Miss Myrtle Mahood of Upland Green, she can ackurately predict the weather by the curliness of her pet pig

Pricilla's tale. "I've never seen old Pricilla's tale so curled up in all my life! This can only meen one thing—we're in for at least half a meter of snow this weak."

That's right, folks! It's hard to beleev, but Pricilla the curly-tailed pig says, as sure as a pig goes "oink," to get out the snow shuvels even thow it's only September.

After reading what Trixi had done to his weather forecast, Martin finally thought of a word to describe how he felt. DIS-GUS-TED! After all those weeks of scientifically reliable weather forecasting, he'd been replaced by a pig's curly tail! Could this paper get any worse?

Of course it could. Way worse.

A WILD AND CRAZY GUY
An Intervue with our crossing gard, Mr. Dogson
by Martun Wettmor

Mr. Dogson, our school crossing gard, is a man with hiden talents. You'd be surprised to lurn that this mild-manered traffic controller is really a sword swalower nicknamed Larry the Leather Larynx.

M.W. How did you furst get into sword swalowing?

Mr. D. Both my father and grandfather were sword swalowers. You might say it was a family tradishun. As a baby, I was given sharp garden tools to teethe on.

M.W. How long were you a full-time sword swalower?

Mr. D. I worked for the Dingling Brothers Circus for twenty years.

M.W. What's your record for most swords swalowed at won time?

Mr. D. Eleven or twelv, depending on how you cownt.

M.W. What do you mean, "depending on how you cownt"?

Mr. D. I actually shoved twelve swords down my throat. But somehow I only pulled out eleven. Go figure.

M.W. Why did you quit sword swalowing?

Mr. D. I had trubble getting through airports with a bag of twelve swords. That's when I desided to become a crosing guard.

M.W. Have you compleetly given up sword swalowing?

Mr. D. Not compleetly. I do a litle on the side. You know, entertane at birthday parties, weddings, bar mitzvahs, that sort of thing. As far as I'm conserned, no special occashun is compleet without a sword swalower.

M.W. I sea. Thanks for taking the time to be intervued. It's been a slice.

A sword swallower? The Leather Larynx? Martin knew that Trixi was sly and underhanded, but she'd reached a new all-time low. She'd changed his reliable, accurate, factual interview into a great big pack of lies! What was Mr. Dobson—not Dogson—going to think when he read this? Martin already knew what Ms. Baumgartner was thinking.

Martin cringed as he turned the page to see what else Trixi had done to his beloved paper.

Enter to win!

Be a bus driver for a day! Yes! You have a chanse to take Mr. Weston's bus for a spin. Drive the morning bus run and

pick up all your frends. But you can't win if you don't enter!
Fill out the entry form below and drop it off, along with $5, at:
Locker #326
Main Hall
Upland Green School

Below the contest entry form was:

TREWTH OR RUMORS?
THE UPLAND GREEN SCHOOL GOSSIP COLUM

It was written by an "anonymous" writer with the initials M.W., who reported that Mr. Quigley, the vice-principal, had started wearing a new brown hairpiece that matched his new glass eye. There was also a rumor that an empty classroom was to be rented out as a rehearsal space to the heavy metal band, Savage Cranium.

Finally, Martin turned to the last page of the paper.

ASK A MARTIAN
UPLAND GREEN SCHOOL'S VERY OUN ADVISE COLUM

Dear Martian,

I've always wanted to make a stink bomb, but I don't know how. Can you tell me the best method?

Sined,
Stinky Wannabe

Dear Stinky,

There are many methods for bilding stink bombs, but I've found the best won to be what I call the "Nuclear Nostril Number." To make it, all you need is...

Martin could almost smell the stench as he read every awful word of the recipe. It finished with this one last piece of advice:

By the way, kids, don't try this at home. It works way better at school!

No wonder Ms. Baumgartner was stinking mad. This edition of the paper was a recipe for disaster.

As he sat in Ms. Baumgartner's office, Martin wondered why *he* should be the one in trouble. Trixi was obviously the one to blame. Surely Ms. Baumgartner could see that. All she had to do was look at all the spelling mistakes. Before Trixi had arrived on the scene, the *Upland Green Examiner* had been full of factual, carefully researched stories. Now it was this...this...this mess of putrefied pulp! It had Trixi Wilder written all over it.

☆ ☆ ☆

While Martin stewed in the principal's office, Trixi was still out in the hall selling papers almost at the speed of light—that is, until Ms. Baumgartner appeared out of the crowd and stood before her.

"Hey, Ms. Baumgartner!" Trixi said. "Just look at the sales

of the paper! It's almost sold out! It sure is an improvement over the old paper, don't you think?"

Ms. Baumgartner scooped the last few copies of the paper off the table and snarled, "In my office. Now!"

When the rest of the kids in line saw that newspaper sales had stopped, they began to chant, "WE WANT A PAPER! WE WANT A PAPER! WE WANT A PAPER!"

Ms. Baumgartner quickly silenced the crowd by shouting, "Enough!" The chanting stopped immediately; everyone knew from the tone of her voice and the look in her eyes that Ms. Baumgartner meant business. The crowd dispersed quickly as Ms. Baumgartner escorted Trixi to the office.

☆ ☆ ☆

While Ms. Baumgartner was out in the hall dealing with Trixi and the crowd, Martin paced back and forth in the principal's office. He knew he was supposed to sit in one of the small yellow chairs, but he was suffering from a bad combination of anger and nervousness. He was furious at Trixi. He was also afraid of what Ms. Baumgartner was thinking. Could she really blame him for this paper when it was obviously Trixi's handiwork? The longer Martin waited for Ms. Baumgartner's return, the more these awful thoughts whirled about in his head. The more his head whirled, the more his stomach churned.

This wasn't good. His rumbling stomach felt like a trampoline with a barrel of nitroglycerin bouncing on it. In his last school, Martin's explosive stomach had earned him the nickname "Barfy." Now he was about to live up to his name once again. His insides were moving toward a large-scale eruption—any second, he was going to upchuck his breakfast and his recess snack.

Martin scrambled around the office, frantically searching for a can or a pail to throw up in. There must be some sort of barf container somewhere. Plenty of kids must throw up in the principal's office. It was a natural thing to do.

After searching every corner of the office, there was no barf bucket to be found. Even the wastebasket wouldn't do, as the sides were made of wire mesh. Time was running out. The situation was becoming critical. He couldn't just throw up on the floor. Only little kids did that. In desperation, just as he was about to throw up, Martin grabbed for something—anything.

Martin yanked open the bottom drawer of Ms. Baumgartner's filing cabinet, hoping it would be empty. It wasn't. The drawer was full of file folders stuffed with papers.

Everything happened very quickly. It was not a pretty sight.

Seconds later, Martin slammed the filing cabinet drawer shut. As he wiped his face with the sleeve of his shirt, the office door swung open and Trixi strode in, flopping down on the other yellow chair.

Ms. Baumgartner looked in through the doorway and said, "Don't move a muscle. Either of you. I'll be back!"

Martin stared at the floor, refusing to look at Trixi. Sure, he was angry at her, but the filing cabinet drawer was a bigger worry right now.

"What's that stench?" Trixi said.

"What stench?" Martin replied quickly.

"Can't you smell that gross stench?"

"No! I don't smell a thing!" Martin said.

"It smells like barf!"

"I don't smell any barf!" Martin said.

What would Ms. Baumgartner do when she charged into her office and smelled the stench of barf? Between the newspaper and the barf in the filing cabinet, Martin's troubles were growing larger by the minute.

But for once, Martin was in luck. Ms. Baumgartner threw open the office door and said, "I've got a couple of kids with bleeding noses out here. I don't have time to deal with you two right now, so come back here right after school."

Martin ran for the door, but as he was leaving the office, he overheard Ms. Baumgartner say to Mrs. Sledge, "I'll need to record the details of these students' injuries. Where do we keep the injury report forms?"

"In the bottom drawer of your filing cabinet, Ms. Baumgartner," the secretary replied.

EIGHT

Trixi sat in class, beaming with pleasure. The new version of the Upland Green school newspaper was a complete success. She knew her version of the paper would sell like crazy. Working on the school newspaper had turned out to be way more fun than anything she'd ever done. It definitely beat washing school buses on Saturday mornings.

Martin sat silently in his class, making plans for an escape from the school. Because of Trixi Wilder, he was in deep trouble with Ms. Baumgartner. And thanks to Trixi Wilder, his newspaper would probably be shut down. Without the newspaper to work on, his mother would make him take babysitting jobs or weed the garden or help Sissy trim the dogs' nails. All because of Trixi Wilder.

First, Martin planned to hitchhike to Bolivia. Then he'd have plastic surgery to change his appearance and assume a new identity. Ms. Baumgartner would never find him, and all the blame for the newspaper would fall in Trixi's lap.

When 3:00 PM finally arrived, Ms. Baumgartner's voice could be heard over the PA in every room of the school and down every hallway. "Martin Wettmore and Trixi Wilder to my office, please."

Martin was still thinking about Bolivia as he trudged down the hall toward the office, walking as if his shoes were filled with concrete. His head, his arms, his shoulders, even his nose and ears felt like limp lifeless rags.

But not Trixi. She swaggered down the hall, her arms swinging back and forth, her head held high. She walked as if she owned the world—including Bolivia.

☆ ☆ ☆

Trixi reached the principal's office first. She found the door wide-open and Ms. Baumgartner sitting behind her desk with her arms tightly crossed and a deep crease running down the center of her forehead. In one hand, she clutched a crumpled copy of the school newspaper.

Trixi slid past the principal and took her place in one of the two yellow chairs. Moments later, Martin shuffled into the office and flopped into the other yellow chair.

"I'm afraid there's only one word I can use to describe this edition of the school newspaper," Ms. Baumgartner said. "Shocking. This paper is absolutely shocking."

"But I thought you said…," Trixi began, but she knew to stop when Ms. Baumgartner raised her hand. The principal was obviously in no mood to argue.

"This…this…newspaper is…is…shocking! That's the only word I can use!" Ms. Baumgartner took a very deep breath. "I asked you to write a school newspaper, not a collection of fairy tales! How do you think Mr. Dobson feels when students ask him to swallow some swords? And the primary students are terrified of the maple trees! As for the instructions for building a stink bomb…I don't think I have to say any more about that!"

As Ms. Baumgartner turned the pages of the paper, she said, "A dog? Driving a car? Snow? In September?"

Trixi had seen Ms. Baumgartner angry many times, but this time, she'd taken her anger to a whole new level. Her nostrils were flared, one of her eyebrows was twitching and the creases in her forehead were deeper than ever.

"But Ms. Baumgartner," Trixi said, "we only did what you asked us to do!"

The principal's eyes widened, and when she spoke, it was in a dangerously calm voice. "What did you say?"

"I said we only did what you asked us to do," Trixi repeated, her eyes never leaving Ms. Baumgartner.

The principal took another deep breath and said, "I certainly did not ask you to write completely untrue stories about vicious trees and sword-swallowing crossing guards! And I most certainly did not tell you to teach our students how to build stink bombs!"

"But you did say you wanted a newspaper the kids at our school would want to buy and read." Trixi kept her eyes on Ms. Baumgartner.

Ms. Baumgartner looked up to the ceiling and sighed. "Yes, I suppose…I suppose that is what I said. But this…this thing you call a newspaper is not what I meant."

"You saw how eager everyone was to buy it," Trixi said. "I'd say this edition of the school newspaper is a great success."

"A success?" Ms. Baumgartner replied, glaring at Trixi.

"Of course it's a success! Everyone loves the new school newspaper. Who can blame them?" Trixi said, jumping out of her chair. Ms. Baumgartner cleared her throat. Trixi sat back down and said, "That article Martin wrote on the dog obedience class? A fine piece of journalism!"

Martin lifted his head for the first time. His eyes were bloodshot, his face streaked with tears.

"And his interview with the crossing guard showed outstanding questioning techniques," Trixi yammered on, not stopping for a breath. "Only a highly skilled reporter such as Martin could write such a wonderful interview!"

Ms. Baumgartner smoothed her copy of the paper on her desk. "As I look at the first article, I count more than twenty spelling mistakes. That's more spelling mistakes than we've had in this paper since Martin began writing it." Ms. Baumgartner stood up and leaned across her desk. "Either Martin's suddenly forgotten how to spell, or someone else wrote these articles without Martin's knowledge."

Martin rubbed his eyes with his shirtsleeves and sat up straight. Even though he hadn't been asked a question, he was nodding his head.

"Spelling, schmelling!" Trixi said. "What's really important? You can't argue with the sales of the paper, Ms. Baumgartner."

"Selling newspapers is one thing, Trixi, but selling lies is an entirely different matter altogether!" Ms. Baumgartner said. "The main purpose of the school newspaper is to inform its readers."

"What good is a newspaper if no one buys it?" Trixi said. "The real purpose of a newspaper is to sell as many copies as possible. And the only way to get people to buy it is with entertainment!"

"Entertainment has its place, Trixi. But you can't take a proper newspaper and turn it into a three-ring circus!"

"People don't want boring facts, Ms. Baumgartner," Trixi said, her voice growing louder. "They want to be entertained! They want excitement! They want gossip! What's wrong with that?"

"What's wrong? What's wrong?" Ms. Baumgartner said, her voice also becoming louder with each word. "Can't you see what's wrong? It might be entertaining, but every last thing you wrote in that paper was made up. It's fiction! It never happened! I was hoping you'd add a bit of pizzazz to the paper, Trixi, not turn it into a pack of lies. That's what—"

Ms. Baumgartner never finished her sentence. The office door blew open. It was the duty teacher, Mrs. O'Reilly. "Ms. Baumgartner, you've got to come quickly! Out on the front field! It's an emergency!"

NINE

Trixi had never seen "Frozen Face" O'Reilly quite like this before. Kids called her that because, from September to June, the expression on her face never changed. Her eyebrows didn't rise when there was a fire in the garbage can. Her lips didn't even twitch the time Trixi cracked a joke that was so funny, five kids fell out of their desks laughing. Her eyes didn't so much as blink when she sat on a whoopee cushion on the bus during a field trip to the game farm.

But today Mrs. O'Reilly's face was twisted into a look of wild, heart-popping panic. Trixi couldn't imagine what it would take to get Mrs. O'Reilly's face to stretch and twist and scrunch like this. Had there been some sort of accident? Maybe someone had been hit by a car! Maybe an airplane had crashed in the soccer field! Maybe an escaped convict was holding a student at gunpoint, demanding a car, a million dollars in unmarked bills and clear passage to the border! Trixi's mind crackled with endless possibilities.

Mrs. O'Reilly grabbed Ms. Baumgartner by the wrist and pulled her out of the office. On her way out, Ms. Baumgartner said, "You two—stay right where you are. I'll be back shortly."

As soon as Mrs. O'Reilly and Ms. Baumgartner were out of the office, Trixi sprang from her chair.

"Hey! Didn't you hear what Ms. Baumgartner just told us?" Martin said. "We're supposed to stay put."

"I am a newspaper reporter. And newspaper reporters must always be on the lookout for new material." Trixi crossed the office to the window and pulled open the blinds. "Oh my goodness! This looks good!" she said. "Really good!" Undoing the latch on the window, she pulled it open and stuck out her head.

Martin couldn't help himself. He slunk across the office to join Trixi at the window. The first thing he saw was Mrs. O'Reilly pulling Ms. Baumgartner across the field toward the maple trees and a great crowd of gasping, shrieking, screaming kids and adults. As Ms. Baumgartner drew closer to the trees, she suddenly took off in a wild sprint, leaving Mrs. O'Reilly behind.

"Can you figure out what's going on?" Trixi said.

"I don't know. I can't really see from here," Martin replied.

"Well, whatever it is, it's too good to miss." Trixi slung her leg up on the windowsill.

"Hey! What are you doing?" Martin took a step back. "We're in enough trouble already!"

"Don't worry, Marty. Ms. Baumgartner's a little busy right now. She won't notice if I'm gone for a few minutes." Trixi slung her other leg over the windowsill, hopped down to the ground and was off across the field.

A few seconds later, Trixi heard Martin shout, "Hey! Wait up!"

When they reached the crowd, Trixi pushed her way through, with Martin close behind. "School newspaper! Let me through!" Trixi said. "Step aside! School newspaper! Let me through!" Once Trixi and Martin had fought their way through the tangle of jostling elbows and shoving hands, they stopped and looked up at a scene that could only be described as bizarre.

There were no injured children, no crumpled airplanes and no escaped convicts. What Trixi and Martin did find was Vice-principal Quigley jumping up and down under the branch of a maple tree. With each frantic jump, he tried to reach a small black clump of hair stuck in a branch about three meters off the ground. Each time he jumped, there was a great flash as the sun glinted off the top of his bald head.

Standing beside Trixi in the crowd was her classmate, Lonnie Blackwell. "Hey, Lonnie. What in the name of Jumping Jack Horner is going on here?"

Lonnie Blackwell had been Citizen of the Year for the last three years. She sang in the church choir, volunteered at the hospital and scraped gum off the bottoms of chairs in her spare time. Lonnie had never told a lie or stretched the truth in her life.

"When Mr. Quigley stepped under the branch, it swooped down like a giant claw and grabbed the hair on the top of his head.

But the hair turned out to be a hairpiece!" Lonnie said. "It was just awful! The hairpiece must have been held on by glue or something, because Mr. Quigley was a little way off the ground before the hairpiece popped off his head and he fell back down. Then the branch just stayed there, holding the hairpiece out of Mr. Quigley's reach."

"You're not serious!" Martin said. "That's the most ridiculous story I've ever heard in my life!"

"But it's true!" Lonnie said.

Martin shook his head and turned to one of his own classmates, Garth Horton. Garth was a member of the Young Astronomers League who liked to spend his Saturdays helping little old ladies cross the street.

"Hey, Garth. I'm hearing some wild stories about what happened here," Martin said. "It looks to me like Mr. Quigley was climbing the tree to rescue a cat and his hairpiece got caught as he was jumping down. That's probably what happened, right?"

"No, it was nothing like that at all," Garth said. "That tree just reached down like it was really angry and yanked Mr. Quigley's hair right off his head! I saw it with my very own eyes!"

"That's ridiculous!" Martin said. "That's impossible! Maple trees are…are…trees! And trees don't do things like that!"

"I guess they do if you read the latest edition of the *Upland Green Gossiper*," Trixi said. She pulled a crumpled edition out of her pocket, held it up and said, "Just take a look at the headline: *THE REVENJ OF THE MAPEL TREES!!! Maple Trees Fite Back After Being Trimed!* And it's actually happening!"

"Don't be ridiculous!" Martin said. "How could some article in that paper have anything to do with this? It's all just a coincidence."

"I wouldn't be so sure about that, Marty. You just never know…," Trixi said with a mischievous grin.

They watched as Ms. Baumgartner wrapped her arms around Mr. Quigley's waist and tried to lift him high enough to reach his hairpiece.

"Maybe we should get back to the office," Martin said.

"Not yet," Trixi said. "Here comes Mrs. Sledge. I figure we're in for a little more action. Let's just wait around to hear what she has to say."

"Excuse me, Ms. Baumgartner!" The school secretary pushed through the crowd and tapped the principal on her shoulder. "There's an urgent telephone call for you."

"Not now, Mrs. Sledge. Can't you see I'm busy?" the principal replied. Mrs. Sledge must have realized that the principal wasn't about to let go of Mr. Quigley, so she wrapped her arms around Mr. Quigley's legs and said, "One, two, three, lift!" The extra boost from Mrs. Sledge was just enough for Mr. Quigley's fingertips to grab his hairpiece.

The crowd cheered as Ms. Baumgartner and Mrs. Sledge let go of the vice-principal. By the time Mr. Quigley hit the ground, Ms. Baumgartner and Mrs. Sledge were already on their way back to the school. Following a few meters behind were Trixi and Martin.

When they reached the window of the principal's office, they climbed back in and returned to their chairs. With the door to the outer office still open, they had a clear view of Ms. Baumgartner as she picked up the phone.

"Oh, hello, Mrs. Reynolds. What can I do for you?" Ms. Baumgartner said.

Trixi could see a puzzled expression come over the principal's face. She pulled the phone away from her ear and rubbed the earpiece with her finger. "I'm sorry, Mrs. Reynolds. We seem to have a bad phone connection. You'll have to speak a little more slowly. I can't understand you."

The puzzled expression remained on Ms. Baumgartner's face. "Did you say *sword swallowing*?" Ms. Baumgartner started rubbing her forehead, a sure sign she didn't quite know what to make of this.

"Are you sure he's our crossing guard, Mrs. Reynolds? I've never heard of such a thing in all my days as a principal."

"Yes, she has heard of such a thing," Trixi whispered to Martin. "She already read about it in the latest edition of the *Upland Green Gossiper*."

"Very well, Mrs. Reynolds. I'll look into it as soon as I can," Ms. Baumgartner said. As soon as she put down the phone, Mrs. Sledge said, "A call for you on line two. It's the police."

"Wow! The police!" Trixi whispered. "Now things are getting really good!"

Martin and Trixi could see Ms. Baumgartner's eyebrows jump as she picked up the phone. "Yes, Constable Jones... I see...I understand your concerns...Yes, a sword swallower would be a traffic hazard. I'll look into it right away...Thank you, Constable Jones."

Trixi giggled as she flipped through her copy of the *Upland Green Gossiper*. "I wonder what's going to happen next?"

Martin sat in his chair, his hands tightly gripping the sides of his head. "It just doesn't make any sense. No sense at all."

"I don't care if it makes sense or not, Marty, but look outside!" Trixi said. "It's snowing!"

Martin pressed his hands over his eyes. "It doesn't snow here in September, Trixi," he said. "I should know. I've studied the weather, and in the history of this town, there's never been a recorded snowfall in the month of September. It must be ashes from a fire or seedpods from some trees or something. It can't be snow."

"Well, it's sticking to the ground, and kids are starting to make snowballs. It looks an awful lot like snow to me," Trixi said.

Martin heard Ms. Baumgartner shouting, "Mr. Barnes! Could you please get the snow shovels out of storage?" He lifted his head and looked out. "This is crazy," he mumbled. A thick blanket of snow covered the ground and was getting deeper by the second.

Students with blue lips staggered about in the blizzard. Cars and school buses were spinning their tires in the parking lot.

Martin and Trixi could hear Ms. Baumgartner on the phone once again, her voice louder than before. "Hello? I need the maintenance department! I need a snowplow to clear our parking lot…Yes, I know it's September!…Yes, I'm sure it's snowing! You can come over and have a look if you don't believe me!"

"I have to say," Trixi said, "the weather forecast in the *Upland Green Gossiper* was pretty accurate."

Martin shook his head. How could his own weather forecast be so wrong? And how could Trixi's weather forecast be so right?

As quickly as the snowstorm started, it stopped. The clouds parted, and once again, skies were blue. Unfortunately, there were now twenty centimeters of snow covering the ground. Cars and buses slid and spun in the wet sloppy snow, and kids who tried to wade through it quickly turned back to the school with cold wet feet.

"Even though it's stopped snowing, no one's going to be able to get home through all that snow," Trixi said. "Ms. Baumgartner's going to have to hold the world's biggest sleepover party. Three hundred kids stuck at school for the night."

"Look!" Martin said. "It's the snowplow!"

But the longer they watched the snowplow, the more Trixi and Martin wondered if this was the snowplow Ms. Baumgartner had requested. Rather than driving in a straight line down the road, it weaved and swerved. It zigzagged across the parking lot, barely missing the teachers' cars. Then it bumped up over the curb, onto the soccer field and around behind the softball backstop, before looping around the swings. Finally, the snowplow began to drive in a straight line. Unfortunately, it was heading straight toward the front door of the school.

With the snowplow only thirty meters from the door, Trixi shouted, "Look! It's Terry Springate's dog, Sparky! He's driving the snowplow!"

Martin couldn't deny what his eyes could clearly see. Behind the windshield of the snowplow, resting on the steering wheel, were the two front paws of a cocker spaniel. The snowplow rumbled across the field in a perfectly straight line, and it didn't look as if Sparky was about to change course.

Trixi and Martin could hear the principal shout, "Clear the front of the school! Everyone out of the way!"

"First a flood in the library, and now a dog driving a snowplow through the front doors of the school. Ms. Baumgartner is having one bad week and a half," Trixi said.

"She wouldn't blame us for this, would she?" Martin said, chewing the fingernails of both hands at once.

But Trixi never gave Martin an answer. A quick glance at Ms. Baumgartner's uneaten bologna sandwich on the principal's desk had given her an idea. She grabbed the sandwich, ran from the office and out the front door.

When Ms. Baumgartner saw Trixi run past her and out into the snow toward the approaching snowplow, she shouted, "Trixi! What are you doing? Get back in the school this instant!"

"It's okay, Ms. Baumgartner," Trixi said. She stopped, knee-deep in the snow, and began waving the bologna sandwich above her head. "Hey, Sparky! Bologna sandwich! Yum! Yum!" Sparky may have been able to drive a snowplow, but Trixi knew he was a dog at heart. When he spotted the sandwich, his eyes opened wide and a wet sloppy tongue flopped out of his mouth. Trixi threw the sandwich as far as she could toward the parking lot. Immediately, Sparky cranked the wheel and turned the snowplow in the direction of the sandwich. He leaped through the window, scooped up the sandwich in his mouth and chomped it down in two bites. The snowplow slowly came to a stop, its front bumper nudging the school's flagpole.

Ms. Baumgartner slapped her hand against her forehead and shook her head. Then she turned to Trixi and whispered in a hoarse voice, "I suppose I should thank you."

"You're welcome, Ms. Baumgartner," Trixi replied as she headed back to the office.

Even though Sparky had cleared some of the snow away, Ms. Baumgartner's troubles were far from over. The temperature rose, and the snow began to melt. Rivers of water rushed to fill the gutters, flood the fields and swamp the storm drains. Within a few minutes, all that was left of the great September snowfall were a few puddles and some sopping, soaking, drenched-to-the-bone students and teachers.

Martin and Trixi were back in the office, sitting obediently in their chairs, when a bedraggled Ms. Baumgartner staggered in, her hair plastered to her head and one of her high heels broken. She stopped and leaned against the doorway with only enough energy to say two words: "Go home."

☆ ☆ ☆

When Martin arrived home, he was met at the door by Sissy and her five dogs.

"Hey, Marty! Is it true? Is it true?" she shouted.

"Is what true?" Martin said.

"I heard a dog was driving a snowplow around the field at the school. And he was smoking a cigar and shouting at everyone in Japanese!"

Martin shook his head and went inside.

"Thank goodness you're safe, Martin!" his mother said. "I heard a terrible story about maple trees pulling people's heads off! I was so worried about you!" Martin shook his head once again and climbed the stairs to his room.

Razor was there, strumming his guitar. "Hey! You decided to come home! I thought you might have been one of the kids who ran away."

"Ran away? What are you talking about?" Martin said.

"To the circus, you twerp! I heard a bunch of kids ran away from the school to join the circus and become sword swallowers."

Martin clasped his hands against the sides of his head and screamed, "I don't believe this! And it's all *her* fault!"

"Whose fault?" Razor said.

Before Martin could reply, his mother shouted from the bottom of the stairs, "Martin! Telephone! For you!"

A look of bewilderment came over Martin's face.

"What did you say?" he shouted back.

"I said it's the telephone! For you!"

"The telephone? For me?" Martin said. He tried to remember the last time anyone phoned for him, but he couldn't. "Are you sure it's for me?"

"Yes, of course I'm sure!" his mother said. "Unless there's another Martin living in this house that I don't know about."

Martin ran down the stairs, jumped over the fifth step and bounded down the hall to the kitchen. Who could it be? What could they want?

He grabbed the phone out of his mother's hand, pressed it against his ear and said, "Who is this?"

"Hey, Marty!" It was a girl's voice. Martin had *never* gotten a phone call from a girl. He didn't say anything. He just pressed the phone harder against his ear.

"Marty? Are you there?"

"Who is this?" he said in a quiet voice.

"Who do you think it is? Queen Elizabeth?" Martin was just about to slam the phone down, when he heard, "It's Trixi, you little doofus!"

His grip tightened around the phone. "What do you want?" he said.

"You're the only person left to call," she said. "All my friends are out, so you were my last resort."

"Last resort? For what?"

"My mom and dad are away at a convention, and our housekeeper's locked in her room watching some reality show finale," Trixi said.

"So?"

"So I had to talk to someone. Especially after what happened today at school. Wasn't that one crazy day? I mean, who would ever believe we'd get that much snow in September? And a dog driving a snowplow? And what about that crazy maple tree? Mr. Quigley better buy stronger glue, if you ask me."

"What do you want?" Martin said.

"What do I want?"

"Yes, what do you want?"

"I don't want anything," Trixi said. "I just thought we could talk about what happened today, that's all."

"That's all?"

"Yeah. That's all. Hey, don't you find that once in a while you're bursting to talk to someone?"

"Not really. I'm not much into talking," Martin said.

"Anyway, did you hear what some of the parents were saying about Mr. Dodson? They were going wild with—"

"The newspaper had nothing to do with it," Martin said.

"What?"

"You're trying to convince me that the newspaper had something to do with what happened today at school," he said. Martin discovered that talking on the phone made him feel braver.

"What? No! I just wanted to talk, that's all," Trixi said.

"I'm kind of busy right now," Martin said. "The dogs' teeth need flossing." Then he hung up.

TEN

At lunch hour the next day, a familiar voice came over the PA system. "Trixi Wilder and Martin Wettmore to my office, please."

Trixi shrugged. She'd been expecting a call from Ms. Baumgartner. The only surprise was that it took until lunchtime. When Trixi arrived in the office, Martin was already there, slumped in one of the yellow plastic chairs. Ms. Baumgartner was behind her desk, chewing on a bologna sandwich.

She seemed calm, but Martin knew what was on Ms. Baumgartner's mind. She was going to blame all of yesterday's chaos and confusion on the school newspaper. She was going to shut down the Upland Green school newspaper.

Trixi also knew what Ms. Baumgartner was thinking. The principal was going to tell her to get ready for an appointment on Saturday morning with some dirty school buses. But Trixi wasn't going to make it easy on Ms. Baumgartner.

She would go on the attack. As soon as she sat down in her yellow plastic chair, she said, "You do realize, Ms. Baumgartner, that it wouldn't look very good if you shut the newspaper down just when it's getting popular."

When Martin heard Trixi's words, a slight sparkle returned to his eyes. Trixi had actually made a strong argument for keeping the paper going. Martin's archenemy had given him a glimmer of hope.

"Trixi, please listen," Ms. Baumgartner said as she put her sandwich down and brushed the crumbs off her hands. "No one's said anything about shutting down the newspaper. But before the next edition, there are a few matters that have to be worked out."

As Ms. Baumgartner spoke, Trixi and Martin both grinned, but for different reasons. Martin was grinning with relief because his school newspaper was still alive. Trixi was grinning because Ms. Baumgartner had been backed into a corner. She knew the principal had no choice but to keep the newspaper going, and Trixi had to be part of it. Her fun was just beginning.

"First of all, the paper will not be called the *Gossiper*," Ms. Baumgartner said. "It will be called by its traditional name, the *Examiner*."

"Ah, come on, Ms. Baumgartner," Trixi said. "The *Examiner* sounds like a newspaper only a doctor would read."

"It always has been called the *Examiner* and will continue to be called the *Examiner*," Ms. Baumgartner said. "Second of all, the stories in the next edition are to be based on facts."

"But all the stories in the last edition were based on facts!" Trixi said. "Everything written in that paper actually happened. Only, they happened after the paper came out, that's all."

"I am not here to discuss the wild events that occurred after the last edition of the paper was published," Ms. Baumgartner said. "Do I make myself clear when I say the stories are to be based on facts?" Martin nodded vigorously. Trixi just smiled.

"Thirdly," the principal continued, "I want to see the next edition of the paper in my office the day before it goes on sale. The paper will only be copied if it meets my approval."

"Whatever happened to freedom of the press?" Trixi said. "I thought we lived in a country where citizens have the right to express their own opinions. Isn't there something in the constitution about that?"

Ms. Baumgartner took a deep breath and spoke slowly. "A newspaper with the school's name across the top, printed on school paper, using the school photocopier, and sold in the school's hallway will be inspected by the school's principal. I'm sorry, Trixi, but that's the way it's going to be. Is that clear?"

Ms. Baumgartner's eyes darted back and forth between Martin and Trixi. Martin was nodding enthusiastically. It looked like the *Upland Green Examiner* would once again be a factual, solid, reliable paper. And who knows? Maybe Trixi would quit if she couldn't have her way.

Trixi wore a smile that Martin knew meant one thing and one thing only: she was already figuring out a way around Ms. Baumgartner's newest set of rules. It was a whole new challenge, and Trixi loved challenges.

"Are we crystal clear on the rules for the next edition of the paper?" Ms. Baumgartner said. Before Trixi or Martin could reply, Mrs. Sledge opened the office door and said, "Ms. Baumgartner! A stink bomb's just gone off in the girls' washroom!"

☆ ☆ ☆

The next Monday at noon, Martin's knees felt a little wobbly as he walked toward his school newspaper meeting with Trixi. His knees shouldn't feel this way. After all, Ms. Baumgartner had given them strict instructions. Martin was the expert on factual reporting, so he was clearly the one in charge. Still, his knees were telling him that he was a little nervous going into this meeting with Trixi the trickster.

When he opened the door to the computer lab, there she was, already sitting at the table, waiting. Martin was short of breath, and he could feel his heart thumping. Why should he be nervous? This was *his* newspaper. It was no time to wimp out.

He didn't sit down. If he did, Trixi would start talking, and she wouldn't stop until she got what she wanted. Martin reached inside his knapsack, and before Trixi could say a word, he pulled out the next edition of the school newspaper and slammed it down on the table.

"It's done!" he said. "The next edition of the *Examiner*. And don't you dare change a word! All you have to do is take it to Ms. Baumgartner, get her approval and make the copies."

He turned quickly to leave, expecting to hear, at the very least, a shout from Trixi, or maybe even feel a pencil hitting him in the back of the head. But he didn't hear or feel a thing. At the door, he hesitated and looked back at her.

Trixi was calmly turning the pages of his paper, carefully reading each story. With every page she read, Trixi nodded and smiled.

"Good," Trixi said. "These stories are so good."

"Yes?" Martin replied. "I mean, Yes! They are factual stories. Just the facts and nothing but the facts. Just what Ms. Baumgartner likes."

"And I like them too!" Trixi said. "Especially this article on the water quality in our drinking fountains. Fascinating."

"Yes. It is fascinating. I was surprised myself at the amount of dissolved oxygen in our drinking water," he said. "Not to mention the levels of turbidity. This story has some shocking details!"

"Oh!" Trixi said. "And an interview with Mrs. Turlington, the substitute teacher. How extraordinary!"

"Yes, I too was amazed to learn about Mrs. Turlington's huge tea-cozy collection."

Trixi read an article about a virus that made half of Mr. Barker's class miss a field trip to the game farm. She also read an article about a marching band that would be performing for the school this week, a story on the grade-six class's pet hamster named Einstein, and, of course, the weather forecast.

Trixi didn't complain, shred the paper into tiny pieces or scream and yell at Martin for writing the worst heap of dullness ever. Instead she said, "There's no doubt, Marty. You've done it again." She straightened the papers so that all the edges were even; then she stood up and said, "I'll be sure to show this to Ms. Baumgartner right away and get her approval." Although these words came out of Trixi's mouth, this did not sound like the Trixi Wilder that Martin knew. A little voice in his head kept telling him that something was wrong. Very wrong. Trixi was never this agreeable.

Just before he left, Martin fumbled inside his knapsack to make sure he had his insurance against any more Trixi Wilder monkey business. He breathed a little more easily when his fingers felt the extra copy he'd made of this week's edition of the *Upland Green Examiner*.

☆ ☆ ☆

The next morning before school, Trixi knocked politely on Ms. Baumgartner's office door. "Oh, excuse me, Ms. Baumgartner, but I have the latest edition of the school newspaper for you to see, just as you requested."

Ms. Baumgartner looked up from her desk and smiled. "Why, thank you, Trixi. I certainly look forward to reading it over. I'm sure you and Martin have done a wonderful job with this week's edition."

Trixi smiled and left the office without another word.

☆ ☆ ☆

For the next twenty-four hours, Martin worried about what trick Trixi might pull with his newspaper this time around. Even though Ms. Baumgartner's new rules were supposedly prank-proof, Martin knew one thing—with Trixi Wilder, anything was possible.

ELEVEN

When Ms. Baumgartner called Trixi down to her office Wednesday morning, everything appeared to be going smoothly.

"You and Martin did a fine job with this week's paper," the principal said. "I read over every page, every line and every word, and I couldn't see one thing that would offend, shock or annoy anyone. All the stories look like they've been carefully researched, plus the spelling and grammar are perfect. Well done!"

"Thank you, Ms. Baumgartner," Trixi said. "But I was just wondering about one thing."

"And what's that, Trixi?"

"Do you think anyone will actually want to buy this paper and read it?"

"We'll just have to see, won't we?" Ms. Baumgartner said. "My main concern is that the stories in the newspaper truly represent our school. And I certainly think this edition does."

"But if we can't sell enough copies, we won't be able to pay for the photocopying, and you'll have to shut the paper down. Isn't that what you told us?" Trixi said.

"Well, certainly. You are absolutely right. The paper must sell enough copies to pay for itself. But let's not worry about that now. You just go ahead with the photocopying, and we'll see how sales go."

Ms. Baumgartner let Trixi into the photocopy room. Before she left, the principal whispered, "I'd suggest not making too many copies, if I were you. You know. Keep your expenses down."

☆ ☆ ☆

Just before recess, Trixi set up a table in the front hall by the office, neatly stacked the copies of the latest edition of the newspaper and placed a tin can with a slot cut in the top beside them. She folded her hands together, rested them on the table and waited.

Martin slipped out of class a minute before the bell and sneaked into the paper-storage room. He left the door open a crack, giving him a perfect view of Trixi and the newspaper sales table. With the sweaty palm of his hand gripping the doorknob, he watched the sale of his newspaper knowing that enough copies had to sell…or else.

When the recess bell sounded, there was a stampede of students pouring out of classrooms and charging down the halls toward Trixi's table. This time, Ms. Baumgartner was prepared. She blew a whistle and shouted, "Anyone who does not line up in an orderly fashion will not be sold a copy of the school newspaper!"

Martin breathed a huge sigh of relief as he watched the lineup grow, stretching straight down the hall, past the library, around the corner and out of sight. Everyone in the lineup was chattering with excitement.

"I can't wait to see what crazy stories they came up with this week!"

"I wonder if there'll be any stories about prehistoric flying reptiles coming back to life!"

"Or maybe an invasion of three-headed alien robots with bad breath!"

"Or how about a pack of crazed zombies out for revenge with deadly rolls of dental floss?"

But when Chucky Wilson, the fifth person in line, bought his copy of the paper and looked at the front page, he spluttered, "What happened to the newspaper? I can't believe it! It's just like the old one! *Water in Drinking Fountains Safe to Drink!* Who wants to pay twenty-five cents to read garbage like that?" Chucky tore up his copy of the paper and threw it down on the table. The first four kids who had bought papers tossed them in the recycle bin, and sales of the paper came to a sudden halt.

☆ ☆ ☆

Word quickly spread down the long line that the school newspaper was back to its boring old self. The lineup scattered.

When Martin saw the crowd leaving, he burst through the door of the paper-storage room and ran down the hall shouting, "Come on, everyone! Give the paper a chance! It'll be the best twenty-five cents you've ever spent! This paper is loaded with good, solid facts! You'll know what really happened around the school last week!"

But everyone in the lineup ran away from Martin as if he really was a zombie armed with a deadly roll of dental floss. In a few seconds, the only ones left in the hall were Martin, Ms. Baumgartner and Trixi.

"Well, it looks like this was the last edition of the *Upland Green Examiner*," Trixi said, drumming her fingers on the stack of unsold copies of the newspaper.

Martin threw his hands up and said, "Doesn't anyone in this school appreciate solid factual reporting? Doesn't anyone want to be properly informed?"

"I guess not," Trixi replied.

Martin pounded the table with his fist. "I know what you're thinking, Trixi Wilder!" Spit flew from his mouth as he spoke. "But that last newspaper you made up wasn't a newspaper at all! It was junk food for the brain!"

"Martin. Calm down," Ms. Baumgartner said. "There's no need to get so…"

Martin was gone. He ran down the hall, into the paper-storage room, and slammed the door.

"Don't worry about him, Ms. Baumgartner," Trixi said. "Knowing Martin, he'll be okay in a while. He just needs some time to himself."

"I suppose you're right, Trixi. We all need time to ourselves once in a while," the principal said. "Why don't you head outside for some fresh air? There's still ten minutes left of recess."

"It's okay, Ms. Baumgartner. I think I'll just stay here. You never know when someone might change their mind and come back for a copy of the paper," Trixi said.

Martin was huddled in the corner of the paper-storage room. Before any horrible thoughts of revenge or escape could fully form in his mind, he heard shouting and screaming out in the front hall. Curiosity got him up off the floor. He pulled the door open a crack and peeked out. It was just like the scene a week ago! A chaotic mess of kids was pushing, pulling, falling over, jumping up—doing everything they could to fight their way toward the table where Trixi was selling the school newspaper.

Ms. Baumgartner was there too. This time, she wasn't quite so worried about crowd control. She stood back and smiled. When she saw Martin coming out of the paper-storage room, she waved him over and said, "It's taken a while, but I think the students finally appreciate your newspaper, Martin. Just look at them!"

Martin had mixed feelings about the scene. Of course, he was happy. His paper was actually selling. He knew his newspaper was good. In fact, this edition might even be great. But he never imagined it could ever be this popular. This was truly amazing.

So amazing that Martin felt a little uneasy. Even though he'd written every word of the newspaper, and Ms. Baumgartner had checked it over, a terrible suspicion crept through his mind. After all, this was Trixi Wilder sitting behind the table selling the newspaper.

"Hey, Martin!" Darcy Brookman shouted. He was across the hall and waving a copy of the newspaper. "You two did it again! I love the story about the drinking fountain!"

Ms. Baumgartner smiled. "I knew they'd find that story fascinating, Martin. Didn't I tell you?"

Jenny Butler, in Mrs. Langley's class, ran up to Ms. Baumgartner with a worried look. "Ms. Baumgartner! I can't stand frogs! They're so icky and slimy, and I just can't stand them!"

"Oh? Is...Is that so, Jenny?" Ms. Baumgartner replied.

Now, Martin was more than suspicious.

"You still have your voice, Ms. Baumgartner!" Darryl Barnard said with a grin.

"Yes, of course I do," she replied. "Why shouldn't I?"

Darryl just snickered.

The principal turned to Martin and said, "What's Darryl talking about, Martin? Why would he ask about my voice?"

"I...I...I have no idea, Ms. Baumgartner," Martin said.

"I hope there's no funny stuff going on with the paper, Martin! I gave the two of you strict instructions!"

Before Martin could say a word, Ms. Baumgartner disappeared into the crowd, fighting her way through the tangle of flailing arms and legs toward the table. When Ms.

Baumgartner's face suddenly appeared out of the crowd, Trixi looked up and grinned.

"As you can see, sales are brisk," she said, leaning on the stack of unsold papers and covering the front page with her arms.

Ms. Baumgartner snapped her fingers three times and pointed at the stack of papers.

"A paper?" Trixi said. "You want to buy a paper, Ms. Baumgartner? It'll cost you fifty cents. The price has gone up because the newspaper's so popular. And we only accept exact change, I'm afraid."

Ms. Baumgartner snapped her fingers again.

Trixi knew the principal wasn't going to budge. She slid her arms slowly off the stack of newspapers to reveal the front-page headline:

DEDLY DRINCKING FOWNTAINS!
Water in school's drincking fowntains contanes sleeping poshon!

Ms. Baumgartner snatched up the newspaper and turned to page two:

MISTERIOUS VIRUS CAUZES ADULTS TO LOOZ
THERE VOICES!

On page three she read:

SCIENCE FARE PROJEC A SUCSESS! GRADE SIX
HAMPSTER IS A GENIUS!

Then there was the weather forecast:

RAYNING CATS AND DOGS? NOPE! JUST FROGS!

Trixi didn't have to wait for Ms. Baumgartner to say anything. She picked up the stack of unsold papers and followed the principal through the crowd to her office. Just before closing her door, Ms. Baumgartner looked at Martin and motioned for him to join them.

Even before Trixi had a chance to sit in her usual yellow plastic chair, Ms. Baumgartner was ranting. "This in NOT the newspaper I approved yesterday! I made myself perfectly clear. The paper I approved was to be copied AS IS and sold AS IS. NO CHANGES! That was clearly plain…er…plainly clear. NO CHANGES!"

"I *did* try to sell the edition of the paper you approved, Ms. Baumgartner," Trixi said, coolly handing her the unsold copies of the *Upland Green Examiner*.

"You saw what happened when we tried to sell Martin's paper," Trixi said. "Five copies sold. Then, after everyone discovered the paper was about as exciting as watching an ice cube melt, no one bought a single copy."

Ms. Baumgartner paced back and forth, her hands held tightly behind her back, her eyes flicking up and down from ceiling to floor and back. Even though she wasn't sure if Ms. Baumgartner was in any mood to listen, Trixi kept talking. "You wanted us to write a paper that would sell. I knew the edition you approved wouldn't sell because it was just so boring. So, last night, I took the stories and did some editing, giving them a bit of punch and pizzazz! Just the way you suggested."

Ms. Baumgartner stopped, stared at Trixi and nodded slowly. Trixi took this as a good sign, so she rambled on. "I knew I couldn't let you down, Ms. Baumgartner! I knew I had to do something to save our school newspaper. So I started selling my punch-and-pizzazz version of the paper. And here are the results!"

Trixi dug into her pants pockets and pulled out handful after handful of coins. By the time her pockets were empty, there was a heap of money on the principal's desk. Ms. Baumgartner slowly walked around to the back of her desk and sat down, her eyes glued to the pile of coins.

"I'm just trying to make the paper pay for itself," Trixi said. "And by the looks of this, I'd say I was pretty successful."

Martin jumped forward and swept his arm across the desk, scattering the coins across the floor.

"Just because you made a lot of money doesn't mean the paper was a success!" he said. His face was turning a scary shade of red.

Trixi shook her head slowly and said, "You're smarter than that, Martin. Everyone knows that the more money you make, the more successful you are. This," she said, pointing at the scattered coins, "means my paper was a success. And yours wasn't."

"But just look at this paper!" Martin grabbed a copy of the *Upland Green Gossiper*. "Who cares if it makes a million dollars? This paper is a disgrace! An embarrassment to the school!"

"Money talks, Marty," Trixi said.

"It's an unfortunate fact, Martin, that the survival of the school newspaper does depend upon it making some money," Ms. Baumgartner said. "Remember our agreement? Enough copies had to be sold to pay for the expenses of copying the paper."

"So, what you're saying," Martin said, "is that it doesn't matter what's written in the paper as long as it sells?"

"No, it's not that simple," Ms. Baumgartner said. "There has to be a—"

Before Ms. Baumgartner could finish, Mrs. O'Reilly appeared once again at the office door.

TWELVE

The last time Mrs. O'Reilly had burst into Ms. Baumgartner's office, she was screaming. This time, she was not. Although her mouth was opening and closing, not a sound came out. She was bug-eyed, her arms flailed and everything about her was screaming. The only thing missing was the actual sound.

"Mrs. O'Reilly! What is it? Say something!" Ms. Baumgartner said.

"Page two!" Trixi said. "Remember? The virus!"

"It has nothing to do with the newspaper," Martin said. "My mom caught laryngitis last month and she sounded…er, didn't sound, just like Mrs. O'Reilly."

Standing alongside Mrs. O'Reilly was one of her students, Cindy Flagstone. Cindy was staring down at the floor, refusing to look the principal in the eye.

It was like a wild game of charades when Mrs. O'Reilly tried to mime why she and Cindy were down at the office as she scurried around the office on all fours.

"A dog? A dog chewed up Cindy's test paper?" Ms. Baumgartner said. "No? A small dog? A Chihuahua? She brought her Chihuahua to school and it attacked the test? It attacked you? No?"

Cindy couldn't stand it any longer. "Einstein wrote my math test for me!"

Mrs. O'Reilly nodded solemnly in agreement.

"Einstein?" Ms. Baumgartner said. "Einstein? We don't have a student in this school named Einstein."

Cindy sighed and said, "Einstein's our class's pet hamster."

Ms. Baumgartner began to rub her forehead again. "Let me get this straight, Cindy. You're saying the class hamster wrote your math test for you?"

Cindy nodded.

"And by a hamster, you mean a small furry rodent that lives in a cage, chews up newspaper and likes to run on a wheel?"

Cindy nodded again, and Mrs. O'Reilly nodded in agreement. Trixi watched Ms. Baumgartner searching for words, for answers, for anything to say about this mystifying situation.

"It's just like the story in this week's paper," Trixi said. "The grade-six hamster really is a genius!"

"I read the newspaper too, Trixi!" Ms. Baumgartner said. "But there's a big difference, young lady, between a fairy tale in the school newspaper and what actually happens in real life."

Mrs. O'Reilly pulled Cindy's test paper out of her pocket

and tapped the paper with her finger, pointing at the *A+* written in red ink across the top. As Mrs. O'Reilly began waving her hands and arms, Cindy said, "She's trying to tell you that I'm not very good at math. I fail most tests." Then Mrs. O'Reilly pointed to a telltale paw print on the edge of the paper.

"The *Upland Green Gossiper* does it again!" Trixi said.

"I wouldn't be so sure, Trixi," Martin said. "This is just another coincidence."

"A math-genius hamster is a coincidence?" Trixi said. "I think not! And it sure isn't a coincidence that Mrs. O'Reilly lost her voice, because I wrote a story about that too. In fact, it looks as if more of the adults have lost their voices!" Three more teachers walked up to the office door, waving their arms and pointing to their throats.

"There you go. What did I tell you? It's true! It's really true!" Trixi said. "A school full of adults who can't talk. Now, that's my idea of paradise!"

Ms. Baumgartner opened her mouth to say something, but nothing came out. She clutched her throat and tried to talk again, but not a sound could be heard. The same could be said—or not said—for Mrs. Sledge.

Ms. Baumgartner ran to her desk and pulled out a pen and notepad. She wrote in a frenzy for a few moments and then held out the paper to Trixi and Martin.

"I can't read her writing," Trixi said. "Here, you read it."

Martin took the notepad and began to read out loud, "*This is an emergency! Are you willing to help?*"

"Sure, I'm willing to help," Trixi said.

"Me too," Martin said.

Ms. Baumgartner took the pad back, scribbled some more and handed the pad back to Martin who read, "I'm calling an emergency assembly. We can't have it in the gym. Some water from the flood seeped into the gym, and today the repairmen are fixing the water damage to the floor. The assembly will have to be held outside on the front field. I'll need one of you to go on the PA to call everyone out to the assembly."

"Really, Ms. Baumgartner? You want one of us to go on the PA?" Trixi said.

Ms. Baumgartner nodded and even added a smile. Trixi couldn't tell if the smile was meant to say *Please do this for me after all the problems you've caused*, or, *I trust you to do the right thing*. Whichever it was, Trixi would take a smile over a frown any day.

"Okay, Ms. Baumgartner. You can count on me," Trixi said.

"Me too," added Martin.

The principal led Trixi and Martin to the microphone. She pressed a few buttons, and then handed the microphone to Trixi, who spoke as if she went on the PA every day of the week.

"Attention, please, students and teachers at Upland Green School! This is an important announcement." Then she handed the microphone to Martin.

"What do I say?" he said. All he got from Ms. Baumgartner was some arm-waving and from Trixi, a mischievous smile. He cleared his throat and put his lips to the microphone. "All classes are to assemble on the front field as poon as sossible… I mean, as soon as possible!"

"As poon as sossible, Marty?" Trixi said. "Where did you learn to talk? Maybe you can write, but when it comes to talking…"

Ms. Baumgartner banged the counter with her knuckles and waved Trixi and Martin back to her office. From a cupboard, she hauled out the megaphone they used on sports day and motioned for Trixi and Martin to follow her outside.

Moments later, the classes began to file out one by one onto the front field and line up just as they would for a fire drill. When the entire school was out, Ms. Baumgartner gave the megaphone to Trixi, along with a clearly written note.

Trixi put the megaphone to her mouth, pressed a button and slowly read, "Thank you all for coming out in such an orderly fashion!" Her garbled voice boomed across the field, and all eyes in the school were upon her. She was loving every moment.

"As with all assemblies," she continued, "we will start by singing the national anthem. Adults are excused from singing for obvious reasons." Everyone rose, stood at attention and waited. But without a piano or a teacher to lead them in the singing, they all just stood at attention, not knowing what to do.

Ms. Baumgartner quickly scribbled a note on her pad and held it up to Trixi. It read, *You start the singing!*

Trixi put the megaphone to her mouth, pushed the button once again and said, "Leading us in the national anthem today will be Martin Wettmore!" She shoved the megaphone in Martin's face and said, "Okay, Marty! Do your thing! It's show time!"

Martin stared out at the six hundred eyes looking back at him. There was nothing else he could do. In a voice that sounded like a cross between a frog and a sick camel, he croaked out the first line of the national anthem. Fortunately, as soon as he began to sing, everyone else with a voice joined in and belted out the anthem with more gusto than ever before.

As the final words of the anthem faded away, twelve students in grade seven yawned and lay down on the ground. A few seconds later, half of a grade-six class did the exact the same thing. Soon students in each and every class were yawning, lying down on the grass and falling fast asleep. Some slept on their backs, folding their hands behind their heads. Others curled up, sleeping with their knees tucked to their chests. One student, Jeremy Horsely, even slept standing up. And of course, there was plenty of snoring.

Only a handful of students—those lucky enough not to have taken a drink from the drinking fountain, remained awake. They gawked with amazement at a field covered in sleeping kids. Although none of the teachers could say anything, they ran frantically from child to child, trying to shake them awake.

Trixi lifted the megaphone to her mouth. "There's no need to panic! If you've read the latest edition of the *Upland Green Gossiper*, you know that our drinking fountains contain a sleeping potion. Any students who drank from the fountains in the school will be asleep for a while. Unfortunately, the article didn't say how to wake them up or how long they'll sleep. Sorry about—"

Martin yanked the megaphone out of Trixi's hands, pressed the button and shouted, "Don't listen to her! It's not true! None of it! The kids are probably just tired from PE class. All they need is a little nap, and they'll be—"

Ms. Baumgartner wrenched the megaphone from Martin, shaking her head solemnly.

"Don't worry, Ms. Baumgartner," Trixi said. "It's not so bad to have these kids sleeping all day. The school's much quieter this way. Teachers like that."

The few kids who weren't sleeping were sent to sit on benches by the school, while Ms. Baumgartner walked up and down the rows of snoozing kids, closely followed by Martin and Trixi. The principal was looking desperately for signs of any snoozing students waking up.

"For your sake, I hope this isn't a Sleeping Beauty sleep, Ms. Baumgartner," Trixi said. "If it is, they'll be sleeping on the front field for a hundred years. And where are you going to find enough handsome princes and princesses to awaken everyone? Princes and princesses are in short supply, you know!"

"Don't worry, Ms. Baumgartner," Martin said. "No one sleeps for a hundred years, except in fairy tales."

"At this rate, they'll probably have to change the name of this place to Rip Van Winkle School," Trixi said.

Ms. Baumgartner kept walking up and down the rows of students, trying to ignore Trixi and Martin. But she couldn't ignore Martin when he suddenly cuffed her on the top of her head. She whirled around and glared at him, giving him a look that was meant to say, "What in the world are you doing?"

"Sorry, Ms. Baumgartner, but you had a frog in your hair. A teeny tiny frog. I was just brushing it off."

"Oh, yuck!" Ms. Baumgartner said. "I can't stand frogs!"

"Hey, Ms. Baumgartner!" Trixi said. "You just talked!"

"I did? Yes! Come to think of it, I did!" Ms. Baumgartner said. "How strange!"

"It's also pretty strange that a frog landed on your head," Martin said. "I've never seen frogs around here before."

"I have a feeling you may see a few more," Trixi said.

She was right. Martin looked up and saw the sky was full of tiny dots. As the dots fell, he could see it was a downpour of frogs—thousands of tiny frogs falling from the sky and croaking up a storm. Everyone who was awake ran for cover. Everyone, that is, except Ms. Baumgartner, Trixi and Martin. They kept on trying to wake up the snoozing students before they were buried in frogs. Up and down the rows they ran, desperately shaking the sleeping kids. Halfway down one of the rows, the three of them stopped.

Above the sound of croaking frogs, they heard a voice squealing, "EEEWWW! Frogs! Two of them landed right on my face! They're so icky!"

It was Jenny Butler. Seconds earlier, she had been snoozing on the grass; now she was wide-awake, on her feet and running for the safety of the school. Soon the air was filled with other sounds of "EEEWWW!" and "GROSS!" and "YUCK!" Kids were jumping up, peeling frogs off their faces and running for cover. The field quickly emptied of snoozing students as croaking frogs fell from the sky.

"If this doesn't let up, we might have to call in a frogplow," Trixi said, as she ran toward the school.

Even though Ms. Baumgartner could now talk, she didn't say a word.

☆ ☆ ☆

When he got home after school, Martin tried to sneak in the back door. But as soon as the hinges of the old door let out their first squeak, his mother flung the door wide-open and squeezed him so hard, Martin thought he heard his ribs crack.

"Thank goodness you're safe! I heard that everyone at your school had fallen into a deep sleep. Someone even said you wouldn't wake up for a hundred years!"

Martin rolled his eyes.

"Don't expect him to say anything, Mom," Sissy called from the kitchen. She was putting nail polish on her poodle, Crusher. "I heard there's some weird contagious disease at the school and everyone's lost their voice. Even some of the neighborhood dogs can't bark."

"Is that true, Martin? Is that true?" his mother said. "Speak to me!"

Razor came down the stairs and shouted, "Nobody move! If that kid's got a hamster, don't let him in the house! I heard we've been invaded by an army of alien hamsters!"

"Is that true, Martin?" his mother said. "Please tell me it isn't true!"

The phone rang and Martin shouted, "Don't answer that!"

It was too late. Sissy had already picked up the phone.

"Hello? Yep, he's here, but you can't talk to him. He lost his voice like all the other kids at school, although I think he might have just said something."

Martin snatched the phone out of Sissy's hand and said, "What do you want?"

"Hey, Marty! It looks like we did it again!"

"Did what again?"

"You were there! You saw what happened!"

"Yes, I saw what happened. So what?"

"Man, are you thick! The paper, of course. Everything we wrote in the paper came true again!"

"*We* did not write the paper. *You* were responsible for that heap of trash. Plus, the paper couldn't possibly have anything to do with what happened at the school."

"You just won't open your eyes, will you, Marty?"

Martin held the phone, not saying a word.

"Hey, Marty! Are you still there? Don't hang up, okay?"

"Why shouldn't I?"

"Well, because…because…because it would be rude," Trixi said.

"I see. So now you're the expert on telephone manners, are you?"

"Yeah, yeah, yeah. I know. I'm not exactly the most polite person, but I've got to talk to someone. And right now, you're it."

"Your parents are still in New York?"

"No, not New York. That was last week. This week, I think they're in Las Vegas or maybe Atlanta. I'm not sure which."

"Ms. Baumgartner's going to shut the newspaper down," Martin said.

"What are you talking about? How could she?"

"I know her," Martin said. "She'll shut the paper down."

"It's not our fault all that stuff happened. How could she blame us? We didn't do anything wrong. Right?…Marty!…Are you there?…Talk to me, Marty!"

THIRTEEN

The next day at 3:00 PM, everyone was in their usual places: Trixi and Martin in their yellow plastic chairs and Ms. Baumgartner sitting behind her desk, her hands clasped together and resting on top of a file folder.

"In our first meeting, I asked the two of you to work together on the school newspaper," Ms. Baumgartner said. "By combining your individual talents, I was hoping you'd create a really good newspaper that students in our school would want to read. I was so hopeful that things would work out."

Martin slumped in his chair, his head flopping forward as if his neck were made of rubber. This time, he knew for sure what was coming.

Trixi sighed every few seconds, impatient with Ms. Baumgartner's need to explain everything. She also knew what was coming.

"I'm afraid, after two tries, things just aren't working out," Ms. Baumgartner said. "The two of you can't seem to work together. Either we get a newspaper no one wants to buy, or we get a trashy tabloid full of outright fiction."

"So I suppose you're shutting the newspaper down," Trixi said.

"I'm afraid that's right, Trixi. The paper just can't continue."

Martin had been sitting motionless, but he flew out of his chair, stood with his hands clenched and shouted, "NOOO! YOU CAN'T DO THIS! THIS IS NOT MY FAULT! THIS IS TOTALLY UNFAIR!" His face was scrunched and twisted, and his body shook with rage.

"Now, calm down, Martin," Ms. Baumgartner said.

But there was no calming Martin Wettmore down. "Do you know how miserable it is to be forced to work on my newspaper with HER?" Little bits of spit flew from his mouth with each *p*, *t* and *b*. "Do you know what it's like to see my newspaper being taken over by HER?" His finger trembled as he jabbed the air toward Trixi. "Then, to top it off, because of HER, my newspaper gets closed down! If you shut the paper down, what am I supposed to do after school every day? Listen to my brother's horrible rock band? Floss my sister's dogs' teeth? Help my mother cook macaroni and cheese for the fifty-fifth night in a row?"

"I'm sorry, Martin. I've given you my reasons. Keeping the newspaper going is out of the question," Ms. Baumgartner said. "I'm sure you could find another hobby, like playing on the basketball team or joining our public-speaking club. You did so well with the megaphone."

"I don't like basketball, and I'm not interested in public speaking. I'm a writer!" Martin said.

"I'm sorry things turned out this way, Martin," Ms. Baumgartner said. "There's nothing more to be said on the matter. You can go now."

"You bet I can go!" Martin said. He ran from the office, and Trixi watched through the window as Martin sprinted across the field, headed for who-knew-where.

Ms. Baumgartner flipped open the file folder on her desk. She took a deep breath before looking up at Trixi. "I was really hoping things would work out differently, Trixi."

"I guess it's school-bus washing for me, right?" Trixi said.

"I'm afraid that's the way it is. I gave you an opportunity, but you refused to work with Martin. Then you disobeyed my instructions by selling a newspaper I hadn't approved."

"I thought you wanted me to write a paper that sold more copies than the old paper. And the only way to get people to buy the paper was to—"

"I know, Trixi," Ms. Baumgartner said, nodding slowly. "But in spite of being warned, you crossed a line with your last paper. You'll be expected at the bus yard at eight on Saturday morning."

Trixi stood up, stepped toward the principal's desk and glared defiantly at Ms. Baumgartner. "Are you doing this because of my parents?"

"Eight o'clock at the bus yard, Trixi. That's all I've got to say to you at this time."

"You're afraid my parents will find out you didn't exactly fix the problem."

"Trixi, that's enough."

"You just want to make it look like you're doing something by punishing me."

"Trixi. I think you'd better leave before you dig yourself into a deeper hole," Ms. Baumgartner said, closing the folder.

Trixi could argue for the rest of the day and night if she had to. But she didn't. Instead she left the office without another word. Trixi preferred action to argument. As she headed out of the office and down the hall, she was already thinking of her next move.

The next morning, Trixi stood on the sidewalk outside the school grounds and waved a newspaper. "Get yer paper here! Special edition of the *Upland Green Gossiper*! Read all about it!"

It didn't take long for a crowd to gather around Trixi and her stack of newspapers. Within minutes, Trixi's special edition was sold out. Everyone wanted to know what weird and wonderful things would be happening that day.

✿ ✿ ✿

Just before the morning bell rang, a small group of kids gathered in the teachers' parking lot and surrounded Ms. Baumgartner's new car.

"I've never seen a swarm of gophers attack anything," Paul Smirl said, looking around the parking lot.

"Do you think gophers can eat metal?" Kelly Brown said. "Or maybe they'll just chew the tires off."

"All I know is I want to be here when it happens," Paul said.

Another group was peering through the window of the staff room.

"That must be the closet over there!" Ingrid Ludwig whispered.

"Are you sure?" Elise Warren said. "That looks like a pretty small closet."

"It's the closest one to the coffee machine," Ingrid said.

Meanwhile, twins Darren and Matthew Archer were pacing around the front field, making bets.

"I think it'll land here," Darren said, digging the heel of his shoe into the ground.

"Naw. There's an easterly wind. It'll blow in this way and land right about"—Matthew ran to the ball diamond and jumped on second base—"here!"

Inside the school, a group of eight kids was standing outside the girls' washroom doors.

"No chance! I'm not goin' in there!" Melissa Watson said, backing away from the door. "Those things are supposed to be the size of a cat, and some might even be bigger!"

"Yuck!" Tasha Walters said. "How are they supposed to get from the toilet into the principal's office?"

"I guess they'll just scoot down the hall," Melissa said.

Trixi's special edition of the *Upland Green Gossiper* was causing both panic and excitement. Excitement and panic for the kids, that is. None of the adults had seen it. They didn't have a clue what was in store for them that day, as copies of the paper were stuffed in knapsacks, crammed into pockets or crumpled into desks. Not one teacher in the school had seen the headline:

PRINCIPLE'S CAR SWORMED BY AINGRY GOFERS!

Nor had they read this:

ANSHENT MUMMY IN STAFF ROOM CLOZET COMES ALIVE AND DRINKS ALL THE TEACHERS' COFEE!

The groundskeeper arrived right after the morning bell to mow the field. He might have had second thoughts if he'd seen a copy of Trixi's paper and read the headline:

TWISTER PICKS UP CAMPGROWND OUTHOWSE DROPS IT ON UPLAND GREEN SCHOOL'S FRONT FEILD!

As for Ms. Baumgartner, she worked away in her office in spite of Trixi's headline:

SEEWER RATS CRAUL OUT OF WASHROOM TOILETS! BUILD NESTS IN THE PRINCIPLE'S OFISE!

All that day, everyone kept their eyes and ears wide-open, watching and waiting for the school to be thrown into total chaos once again. For the teachers, it was a pleasant change from the normal buzz of chattering students. No one said a single word. It was that quiet.

One of those silent students was Trixi Wilder. She just grinned, leaned back in her chair and waited for her grand plan to unfold.

☆ ☆ ☆

Martin Wettmore didn't know a thing about Trixi's special edition of the *Upland Green Gossiper*. The day after his meeting with Ms. Baumgartner Martin stayed in bed, pretending he had the flu. He spent his whole miserable day with an image of Ms. Baumgartner in his head; swirling around her were words like *unreasonable*, *thoughtless, mean* and *unfair*.

Martin didn't care that the electricity in the house was off all day or that Razor and five of his friends had skipped school to play floor hockey in the hall outside his room. He didn't flinch when three of Sissy's dogs jumped up on his bed and had a fight. He didn't open his eyes when one of Razor's friends let off a firecracker in the upstairs bathroom or when his mother came home early from work and played her Barry Manilow CD full blast seven times in a row. Martin was a bag of misery.

☆ ☆ ☆

At Upland Green School, every student in every classroom held their breath and waited. At the sound of the recess bell, a herd of kids stampeded out to the parking lot. There was great disappointment when they saw that no chunks of metal had been bitten off Ms. Baumgartner's car. There weren't even any scratches on the paint, and not one tooth mark could be found on the bumpers. Not one single sign of angry gophers whatsoever.

"Hey, Trixi!" Paul Smirl shouted. "I thought your paper said some angry gophers would—"

"I know, I know, I know," Trixi said. "Just be patient. Have any of my newspapers ever let you down?"

A line of kids stood around the edge of the field looking up, keeping their eyes peeled for flying outhouses. All they saw were a crow and two chickadees.

Another crowd cupped their hands against the glass of the staffroom window. The closest thing to a mummy they saw was Mrs. Kensington, the grade-seven teacher, in a wraparound dress she'd brought back from her trip to Thailand.

"Hey, Trixi! Are you trying to make us look like a bunch of idiots?" Megan Tomlinson said. "Where's the mummy?"

"These things take time," Trixi replied. "You've got to wait and watch. But I guarantee, it'll be worth it!"

No one dared go into the washrooms. Everyone was too terrified of coming face to face with a sopping wet, cat-sized, sewer rat running from a toilet bowl to the principal's office. There were plenty of kids standing around crossing their legs and making strange faces, but no one went inside. No one, that is, except for Sally Sweeny.

On her way to school that morning, Sally had guzzled three extra-large Slushies-in-a-Barrel from the convenience store down the street. As she stood outside the girls' washroom at recess, Sally knew she could either wet her pants or confront the sewer rats. The crowd around the girls' washroom gasped when Sally charged through the door and disappeared inside.

"Sally! Watch out!" Laura Birken yelled. "You'd better come out, 'cause no one's coming in to save you!"

There was no reply. The door remained closed. Standing in complete silence, everyone listened. They were expecting to hear Sally howling as the gigantic sewer rats leaped out of the toilets and surrounded her. They were expecting to hear Sally shriek and scream when the rats sank their massive teeth into her leg. But they heard neither howling nor shrieking nor even one solitary scream. Moments later, Sally casually strolled out the door.

"What about the sewer rats?" Laura said. "How big were they? How many were there?"

"The only thing I saw was a crumpled paper towel on the floor," Sally said.

"That's it?" Laura said. "No bloodthirsty foot-long rats with razor-sharp teeth and really bad personalities?"

"Nope," was all Sally said.

Recess passed. Lunch went by. When the end of the school day arrived, not one single story written in the pages of Trixi's special edition had come true. You could smell the disappointment in the school.

As everyone filed past her in the hall on their way home, Trixi shouted, "By Monday morning, everything will have happened! I promise! Just you wait! You'll see!" But no one said a word to Trixi. They didn't have to. Their dirty looks told her exactly what they were thinking.

When everyone was gone, Trixi plodded out the door and headed home to an empty house. As she walked, she racked her brains, trying to figure out what had gone wrong. Why hadn't the stories in her special edition come true?

FOURTEEN

At home that night, Trixi sat under the pink canopy on her pink bed and flipped through the channels on her bedroom TV. But her mind was not on the images flashing by on the giant screen. Her mind was busy trying to figure out what had gone wrong with her special edition of the *Upland Green Gossiper*.

She had tried to phone her parents, but all she got was her mother's recorded voice telling her to leave a message. Then Trixi had called Alyssa and Megan and Marcie and Jenny and Brianne. But each of them hung up as soon as they heard her voice.

Then she knocked on Mrs. Primrose's door, but the house-keeper was watching the finale of *Juggling with the Stars*, so she couldn't be disturbed for the next two hours.

Trixi even tried to phone Martin, but no one answered. With no one to talk to, Trixi decided to get her mind off her horrible day by watching TV. The things that had happened that day—or the things that *hadn't* happened—kept replaying in her mind.

Why hadn't the gophers come through for her? Where was that flying outhouse when she needed it?

At 11:00 PM, Mrs. Primrose pounded on her door. "Shut that television off and turn out the lights. And I mean now!"

As Trixi lay in the darkness, she stared up at the glowing stars and planets stuck to her ceiling, trying to forget everything and get to sleep. But in a clump of stars right above her bed, she could see the shape of a rat. It was the exact shape of the sewer rats that were supposed to climb out of the toilets at school. But they never showed up.

To the right of the rat, another group of stars took on the shape of a mummy. The longer she looked, the more it looked like the mummy was holding up a coffee cup to its mouth. She'd seen this mummy before in her imagination as she was writing the latest edition of the paper. But where was that mummy when she really needed it?

Trixi turned on her side. Instead of facing up at the stars on the ceiling, she was staring straight at her clock radio. She watched the minutes slowly tick by, crawling into hours.

At 7:00 AM, Mrs. Primrose banged on her door and shouted, "Time to wake up!" But Trixi had never fallen asleep.

✧ ✧ ✧

That evening, Martin received five anonymous phone calls.

"What kind of newspaper are you and Wilder printing, huh?" a voice screamed over the phone. "We didn't see one single coffee-drinking mummy! And where were the flying outhouses? And what about the car-eating gophers? Nothing happened! Nothing!"

The four other phone calls were much the same. All angry, all talking about things Martin knew nothing about. But after the fifth phone call, he had a pretty good idea of what had happened at school that day. He yanked the phone cord hard enough for the phone jack to pop out of the wall. Now, no one could remind him of school and of the newspaper which no longer existed.

Just before he went to bed, Martin's mother called him into the kitchen. Mountains of miniature cucumbers and piles of dill weed covered the counters. "Martin," she said over a bubbling pot, "all this moping around the house pretending to be sick will end tomorrow. No matter what, you are going to school. I'm not leaving you at home alone, and I don't want to miss work a second day in a row."

Martin didn't bother telling his mother that tomorrow was Saturday. He trudged up to his room and flopped onto the bed. He didn't brush his teeth or change into his pajamas. He just lay there, awake…wide-awake, staring at the street-light outside his window. The only sound in the room was the bubbling of Razor's piranha tank. He listened for the whistle of the 11:07 freight train, but it never arrived. Razor stumbled into the room at 11:45, dove onto his bed and fell asleep instantly. He didn't even snore. The 1:42 freight train that usually made the windows rattle and the floor vibrate never came by. There were no fires and no sirens that night.

In all of this silence, Martin lay wide-awake, his eyes closed, but his mind wide-open. How could Ms. Baumgartner even think of shutting his newspaper down? How could she be so unfair? These two questions cycled through his mind over and over, with no answer to stop them.

At 7:00 AM, his mother banged on his door and shouted, "Martin! Time to get up for school!" But he was already wide-awake.

Just like any weekday morning, he washed, ate breakfast, grabbed his backpack and headed out the door. He still hadn't bothered telling his mother it was Saturday. It didn't matter. As long as he was out of the house, she'd be happy. As Martin closed the back door and walked down the creaky steps, he thought about where he could spend the day.

When Trixi turned up at the bus yard at exactly 8:00 AM, someone was already hosing down one of the school buses. She could hear the thrum of a power washer and the rumble of a jet of water hitting the side of the bus. As she walked around the edge of the fence and through the gate, she stopped and shouted, "Hey! Did Baumgartner make you come and wash school buses too?"

Martin cut the spray from the hose and picked up a bucket of sudsy water, moving to the rear of the bus. "Ms. Baumgartner told me to look for a new hobby. This is it."

"You call this a hobby? I call it punishment. Why don't you take up something more fun like picking up litter or writing lines?"

Martin picked up the power-washer nozzle and fingered the trigger. It was so tempting. Instead he said, "How do you know I don't enjoy washing school buses? Maybe I like blasting hunks of mud with powerful jets of water."

"Sure. Maybe you do, but it's not my idea of a good time," Trixi said. "Still, it's not like I've got a choice. I'm stuck doing this stupid job."

"I'm surprised you didn't put any stories in your paper yesterday about automatic bus-washing machines," Martin said.

"You heard about the paper, huh?"

"Indirectly," Martin said. "I had a few phone calls from some of your friends. They thought I was involved in your last edition. I gather things didn't turn out all that well."

"I'll say. The special edition was about as special as a moldy sock. Not one thing happened the way it was supposed to. Not a single one."

"This must be the first time a prank of yours has backfired."

"You got that right," Trixi said. "And the worst part is that Baumgartner really deserved everything I wrote in that paper."

"I'll say. I've never met a principal who was so unfair," Martin said. He pointed the power washer at the school bus and pulled the trigger, blasting the back window.

"You know what's really weird?" Trixi said. "You and I finally agree on something."

"Yeah, that's pretty strange," Martin said.

"Well, I guess I'd better start work. If I'm late, Baumgartner'll probably add another week to my sentence," Trixi said, taking the power-washer nozzle from Martin.

As she began to spray down the tires, Martin said, "So, after the flop of your last paper, are you having second thoughts about the first two papers?"

"What do you mean?" Trixi said.

"Do you still think all the weird stuff that happened at school was caused by the newspapers?"

"Yeah. Of course it was." Trixi stopped the spray and looked at Martin. "Don't tell me you still think it was a coincidence."

Martin took the soppy sponge out of the bucket of soapy water and squeezed it hard with both hands. "I'm thinking… I'm thinking that something very weird was going on," he said.

"So you actually admit that the newspaper caused all that craziness?" Trixi said.

"I didn't want to believe it at first. But after the second time it happened, even I have to admit there must be some sort of connection," Martin said.

"But I can't figure out why none of the stories came true yesterday," Trixi said. She gunned the power washer and sprayed it back and forth over the windows. "I tried to do everything the same with the newspaper, but something went wrong along the way."

Martin dunked the sponge in the bucket and began to wash the taillights. "Did you use the same computer?" Martin said.

"Yep. Same computer."

Martin paused and plunged the sponge back in the bucket. "Maybe you used a different type of paper or different fonts or something."

"Nope. I tried to make sure everything was the exactly same."

"Hmm. That is strange," Martin said. He picked up his bucket and moved to the front of the bus. "Maybe it had something to do with when you copied it. What time of day was it?"

"Early in the morning. I did it in my mom's office before our housekeeper brought me to school."

"You copied it in your mom's office?" Martin squeezed the sponge, the soapy water dribbling onto his shoes.

"Yeah." Trixi let the spray of water arc over the roof of the bus.

"You didn't use the school photocopier?"

"Well, duh! Do you think Baumgartner would let me copy my own paper on the school's photocopier?"

Trixi cut the sprayer and stared at Martin.

"It's got to be the photocopier!" Martin shouted as he threw the sponge against the windshield, leaving a soapy smudge in the middle of the glass.

"Yeah! The photocopier!" Trixi said. "It's the only thing that's different!"

"I hate to say this," Martin said, "but in a weird sort of way, it makes sense. After folding origami animals, filling in test answers and translating everything into Japanese, this sort of thing shouldn't be a surprise."

"Of course, it's the photocopier!" Trixi said, spraying a jet of water straight up in the air. "Why didn't I think of it earlier? If I could just reprint that special edition of the *Gossiper*, then Baumgartner would finally get what she deserves! But she's probably got that photocopy room locked up tighter than Fort Knox."

A huge grin blossomed across Martin's face as water rained down from above.

"Why the idiotic grin?" Trixi said.

"When I used to copy the newspaper, I would go early in the morning before all the teachers arrived. That way, I wouldn't be printing the school newspaper when all the teachers wanted to use the photocopier."

"Yeah? So? What are you getting at?"

"To get into the photocopy room, Ms. Baumgartner gave me this…" Martin reached into his soaked shirt and pulled at a string tied around his neck. On the end of the string dangled a key. "She didn't ask for it back when she shut down the newspaper."

"You have a key to the photocopy room?" Trixi said. She let the power-washer nozzle clatter to the ground. "Let me have it, and I'll sneak in and—"

"Not so fast," Martin said, shoving the key back into his shirt. "Before any more copies of the school newspaper get printed, I want to have a say in what stories are in it."

"Ah, come on, Marty! The *Gossiper* isn't your kind of paper," Trixi said, throwing her hands up. "There's none of that factual mumbo jumbo. The *Gossiper*'s all about having some fun and stirring things up in the school. You know, give Baumgartner a headache or two."

"I know exactly what kind of a paper the *Gossiper* is," Martin said.

"Marty, listen. If we're going to take the chance of sneaking into the photocopy room, we've got to write a paper that's really good. I mean REALLY good, like sewer rats and mummies and flying outhouses. Stuff like that!"

"I'll admit that the stories in my newspapers weren't all that exciting. That's why we have to work together."

"What do you mean work together? You're beginning to sound like Baumgartner!"

"So what? The point is you want your newspaper to cause all kinds of trouble in the school. But I'm the one with the key to the photocopy room. If you want to use my key, you have to let me work on the next edition of the paper."

Trixi sighed. "Why would we bother to write another paper when I have a perfectly fantastic edition ready to copy?"

"Because instead of using the next edition of the school newspaper to *make* problems for Ms. Baumgartner, we could use it to *solve* her problems."

"That doesn't sound like any fun at all. Why would we want to do something like that?"

"Why, Trixi? Because you're washing school buses on Saturday mornings, and I don't have my school newspaper anymore. That's why."

"But those are the very reasons why we should make a bunch of trouble. It's called *revenge*, Marty."

"All revenge will do is get you washing more school buses, and it certainly won't bring my newspaper back. Instead we'll use the paper to get ourselves *out* of trouble," Martin said.

"How are we supposed to do that?"

"You're the ideas person, Trixi. Just think about it for a second. Other than us, what's the biggest problem Ms. Baumgartner has right now? The library, right?"

"Yeah, I guess so."

"So, you and I use the paper to help rebuild the library. We'll become instant heroes! And when we're school heroes, Ms. Baumgartner will have to take you off bus-washing duty, and she'll have to let me run my newspaper again!"

"But causing trouble's way more fun," Trixi said.

"Maybe so, but where will it get you? If you cause any more trouble around here, Ms. Baumgartner will probably have you washing every car in town six days a week."

"You may have a point there," Trixi said. "But before I agree to anything, I've got to hear every detail of your little scheme."

"Okay, here's what I'm thinking. Next week is the Fall Fair Fundraiser..."

✿ ✿ ✿

Trixi listened to the rest of Martin's plan and said, "As the queen of wild and crazy ideas, I have to hand it to you, Marty—your plan doesn't sound too shabby. It might even work. Then again, if it doesn't work, it was all your idea."

FIFTEEN

On Saturday night, a shadowy figure crossed the railway tracks, skulked up the lane past the fire station and went through the back gate of a ramshackle old house. When the gate swung shut, there was a chorus of yelping and yapping. The porch light flickered on; then suddenly all the lights in the house went out. The back door creaked open, and a flashlight shone down on a person standing at the bottom of the stairs.

"Come on in. Don't worry. The power usually comes back on after a while."

Trixi walked up the wobbly steps to the back door. As soon as she stepped into the kitchen, five dogs leaped up at her, followed by five long slobbery tongues, licking her hands and face.

"You've…got…really…friendly…dogs, Marty," Trixi said.

"They're my sister's dogs. Just ignore them," Martin said. "Follow me."

Trixi pushed the dogs away and followed Martin through the kitchen.

"Someone must like cucumbers," Trixi said, walking around dozens of boxes of miniature cucumbers stacked around the kitchen.

"My mom. She makes her own jars of pickles and sells them at the farmers' market. The ones she doesn't sell, we have to eat."

"Yummy," Trixi said. "I love pickles."

"You wouldn't love pickles if you had them in your breakfast cereal, on your sandwiches at lunch, and cut up in your macaroni for dinner. I am so sick of pickles!"

"What's that funny burning smell?" Trixi said.

"My sister's trying to bake dog treats. We're lucky the power went off," Martin said. "She specializes in charcoal-flavored dog treats. Not even dogs'll eat them."

Trixi followed Martin up a dark narrow staircase that creaked and groaned with each step.

"Don't lean on the handrail," Martin said. "My brother just stuck it back on the wall with duct tape. And watch the fifth step. My brother accidentally broke it with an axe."

Trixi was feeling her way up the stairs when the lights suddenly flicked back on. Along with the lights, came a blast of sound that made the walls and floor vibrate.

"WHAT IS THAT?" Trixi shouted.

"RAZOR!" Martin said.

"WHAT? A RAZOR? THAT'S AN AWFULLY LOUD RAZOR!"

"RAZOR'S MY BROTHER! IT'S HIS NEW SOUND SYSTEM! HE LIKES HIS MUSIC LOUD!"

"I CAN TELL!"

When Martin bumped the bedroom door open with his shoulder, the music got even louder. Martin shouted, and a deeper gruffer voice yelled something back. Seconds later, the music was turned down.

Martin poked his head out the door and said, "Come on in."

"What about Razor?"

"He's gone."

"Gone?" Trixi said, peering through the door. "Where'd he go? Out the window?"

"Yeah. He figures it's safer to jump off the garage roof than to use the stairs."

Over the next two hours, Martin and Trixi sat in front of Martin's computer, working on their extra special edition of the Upland Green school newspaper. During that time, the power went off twice, two of Sissy's dogs peed on the floor and the fire department roared off to answer three calls. Two freight trains rumbled by and the smoke detector screeched when Sissy baked her next batch of dog treats.

As Trixi left, stepping carefully down the back stairs, she said, "Maybe tomorrow night we should work on the newspaper at my place."

☆ ☆ ☆

As Martin stepped onto the walkway leading up to Trixi's house, the intruder alarm howled. High-powered spotlights shone from all directions. He froze, waiting for the attack dogs or maybe even machine-gun fire. But when he didn't hear any growling dogs or gunfire, he began to walk very cautiously toward the house. After five steps, he heard a strange hissing sound. The lawn sprinklers switched on and sprayed from every direction.

Martin sprinted to the front door and hammered at the solid oak with his fist. The door swung open, and he tumbled across the shiny monkeywood floor. When Martin looked up, he saw a tall woman in a black uniform glaring down at him.

"What is the meaning of this, young man?"

"It's okay, Mrs. Primrose!" Trixi called from down the hall. "It's Martin, and he's come to work on a project with me."

"Work on a project, Beatrix? With this boy?" she snorted.

Trixi waved for Martin to come into the family room. Then she closed the door and pulled up an extra chair to the computer desk. But Martin was still standing across the room by the door.

"Who was that?" Martin said.

"Ah, don't worry about her. She's our housekeeper. She takes care of the house and me so my parents can concentrate on their careers."

"Oh," Martin said. "Do you like her?"

"It doesn't really matter if I like her. My parents like her because they say she has *high standards*."

"Oh," Martin replied.

"Come on. We'd better get down to work," Trixi said. "We've got a newspaper to write."

✩ ✩ ✩

Wednesday night at 7:00 PM, Martin stood outside the school's staffroom window. Inside, he could see the night janitor, Mr. Meeker, sitting at a table eating his dinner of pickled herring on rye bread. Martin knocked on the window and began to wave his arms crazily. Mr. Meeker put down his sandwich and headed for the front door. Pulling it open a crack, Mr. Meeker grunted, "What ya want, boy?"

"It's an emergency!" Martin said. "I was swinging on the swings, and now I have to go to the bathroom! All of a sudden! Right this minute! Now!"

Before Mr. Meeker could say a word, Martin pushed the door open and ran in.

"You be quick, now!" Mr. Meeker said.

Halfway down the hall, Martin glanced back to make sure the custodian had returned to his pickled-herring sandwich. He ran right past the washroom and straight to the back door. Martin popped the door open and let Trixi into the school. Together, they sneaked down the hall and straight to the photocopy room. As they stood outside the door, Martin tugged at the string hanging around his neck, and out came the glittering photocopy-room key.

Nine minutes later, the door to the photocopy room flew open. Trixi and Martin ran out, followed by billowing clouds of black smoke and the stench of melting plastic. They were out the back door and into the dark night by the time Mr. Meeker had swallowed his last bite of pickled herring.

☆ ☆ ☆

The next day at school, Trixi and Martin arrived with the *Extra Special Edition of the Upland Green Gossiper.*

"We've got to do things exactly the same as we did with the first two editions of the *Gossiper,*" Martin said. "We don't want to take a chance by changing anything and messing it all up."

"I still think it's great you let me call it the *Gossiper,*" Trixi said.

Martin shook his head and said, "Remember. Exactly the same."

"Right," Trixi said. "What about selling them in the front hall? How's that going to work? Baumgartner would be on to us in no time."

"You're right. We'll have to take our chances and hand them out," Martin said. "In secret."

"Why in secret?" Trixi said.

"It's just a feeling I have. I don't think we should be advertising our great plan to save the library. Let's just see what happens."

"Good thinking," Trixi said.

That morning, they slipped one copy into Tanis Carswell's open locker, stuffed a copy into Karla Noseworthy's desk, put one copy into Jason Drury's lunch box and slid a copy between the pages of Rob Waxman's math book.

Four copies of the *Extra Special Edition of the Upland Green Gossiper* were out there for anyone and everyone to read—if they could find them.

But Tanis stayed home that day with a bad case of chickenpox. Karla stuffed her science textbook into her desk and jammed the newspaper into the back corner. Jason's juice box sprang a leak and soaked everything in his lunch box, turning it into a pulpy, mushy, gooey mess that ended up in the dumpster. Rob hated math, so the last book he would ever open was his math textbook.

After she'd handed out four copies of the latest edition of the school newspaper, Trixi went by the office to give Ms. Baumgartner a note from the bus-yard supervisor that confirmed her attendance last Saturday morning. As she reached the doorway, she heard the principal say, "Step aside, everyone! Please move out of the way." Coming down the hallway from the photocopy room, Ms. Baumgartner and Mr. Barnes, the custodian, were pulling a trolley. Loaded on top of the trolley, Trixi saw what was left of the photocopier—its plastic sides melted and covered in black soot.

"A problem with the photocopier, Ms. Baumgartner?" Trixi said.

"I've never been able to figure this machine out. It was working just fine when I left last night, but when I came in this morning, it was a burnt-out stinky hunk of melted plastic. It looks like the remains of some ritual sacrifice!"

"That is really strange," Trixi said.

"And of course it would have to happen on the day of the Fall Fair Fundraiser! I've got a million things to organize before tonight. It seems to be one thing after another these days!"

Ms. Baumgartner, with the help of Mrs. Sledge and Mr. Barnes, continued out of the office and through the front door to where a flatbed truck was waiting to cart the old photocopier away.

The office was empty. Trixi just couldn't resist. She tiptoed into Ms. Baumgartner's office and left the note from the bus-yard supervisor on her chair. Then, underneath a stack of file folders on top of Ms. Baumgartner's desk, she slipped the last copy of the *Extra Special Edition of the Upland Green Gossiper.*

SIXTEEN

When the doors opened for the Fall Fair Fundraiser, a crowd rushed through the halls to every corner of the school. Among the crowd were Trixi Wilder and Martin Wettmore.

"Let's hit the gym first," Trixi said. "I figure something big'll probably happen there first."

"Good idea," Martin said.

When they entered the gym, everything looked completely normal. Just like every other year, games were set up around the outside edge of the gym. For twenty-five cents, you could try to sink a basketball, toss a ring over a bottle, throw a dart to pop a balloon or, for the little kids, cast a line in the Fish Pond.

"It looks like the only thing they're catching at the Fish Pond are pink hair-clips and plastic dinosaurs," Trixi said.

"Give it some time," Martin said. "There's still two and a half hours to go."

They headed across the gym to one of the most popular activities—the Dunk Tank.

"Wally Lumkowski's not supposed to be sitting in the dunk tank!" Trixi said. "It's supposed to be—"

"I know, I know," Martin said. "Be patient. I'm sure our special guest will be here soon."

"I don't know," Trixi said. "Things look way too normal for my liking."

"Give it some time," Martin said. "In the meantime, why don't we check out the Bingo room?"

When they looked in the Bingo room, it was only half-full. Mrs. Donnelly was selling cards while Mr. Burns called out the numbers just as they did every year.

"Way, way too normal," Trixi said, checking her watch.

"There's always the auction," Martin said. "For some reason, I have a good feeling about the auction."

When they arrived in the music room where the auction was being held, someone had just bid twelve dollars for a deluxe pizza from Peter Pepper's Pizzarama.

"Twelve bucks for a pizza! That's horribly, horribly normal!" Trixi said.

"Let's wait around for the next item. I think we're on the verge of something big here!" Martin said.

Next up for auction was a truckload of firewood. When the auctioneer's gavel hit the podium, he shouted, "Sold! For ninety dollars to the man in the blue sweater. What a bargain!"

Now, even Martin was looking worried. "I wonder if we did something wrong?"

"Of course we did something wrong! Everything's way too normal! Nothing we wrote in that stupid paper is happening!" Trixi said.

"Maybe we should have—," Martin began, but Trixi was already gone, down the hall to check out the only room left—the Cake Walk.

"This is our last hope," she said, as they peered in through the door of the Cake Walk room. All they saw was a bunch of kids, marching around in a circle while music played, hoping to win one of the prize cakes.

Trixi shook her head and tapped her watch. "It's already seven o'clock. It's been half an hour and I've seen zippo. Not one single thing we wrote in that stupid little newspaper has happened."

"There's still a couple of hours to go before it's over," Martin said.

Trixi jabbed Martin in the chest with her finger. "I knew I never should have listened to your dumb idea. I'm the ideas person around here—not you! And I wasted all that time doing extra writing for nothing. It wasn't even a school assignment. I could have been doing something fun instead."

"Like what?" Martin said.

"What do you mean, like what?"

"What would be more fun than working on the newspaper?"

"Well…" Trixi looked up at the ceiling. "Well, certainly not washing school buses. I hate that. And definitely not shopping with my mom. That's no fun because she always makes me buy stuff I don't like."

"But I asked you what would be *more* fun than working on the school newspaper," Martin said. "I'm no expert, but I sort of thought you were having some fun making up all those wacky stories."

"While you corrected my spelling," Trixi added.

"Well, yeah. That's my job," Martin said. "You're the one who's supposed to come up with all the crazy stuff. And you did."

"Yeah. I guess I did," Trixi said. "I guess even if nothing happens, the stories in that paper are pretty great. So, maybe I guess it was kind of fun in a weird sort of way. I guess."

"Too bad our plan didn't work out, but we didn't have much to lose," Martin said. "Good thing Ms. Baumgartner'll never hear about our *Extra Special Edition of the Upland Green Gossiper*. If she found out we printed up another edition of the school newspaper without her permission, she'd blow the roof off the school! She'd probably blast us into orbit and have us washing the international space station!"

Trixi stood motionless, except for her eyes. They were flitting left, right, up, down—just like the thoughts bouncing around in her head.

"Martin, do you know where Ms. Baumgartner is right now?" she said.

"The last time I saw her, I think she was in the gym, trying to get people to buy tickets for the Dunk Tank. Why?"

"No reason. No reason at all. I've just got to run down to the office for a minute. I'll be back!"

Trixi whirled around and began to sprint down the hall.

But only four strides into her run, she smacked right into a kid leaving the Cake Walk. It was Ryan Padget who was carefully balancing the triple-decker chocolate cake he'd just won one minute ago.

The two of them tumbled to the floor in a tangle of arms, legs and triple-decker chocolate cake. Ryan got his first mouthful of that delicious cake when he hit face-first into the top layer. Cake was smeared all over the floor, with Ryan's face covered in clumps of icing. He coughed, gagged and spat out wads of soggy chocolate. On one final spit, something small, hard and sparkly clattered across the floor. Ryan reached over and picked it up. "Hey! This cake had a prize inside! It looks like…"

"A DIAMOND RING! A REAL DIAMOND RING!" Trixi screamed. "It worked! It really worked!"

"I don't believe it," Martin said.

"Gwennie came through for us, after all!" Trixi said.

A crowd of people thundered down the hall to see what the screaming was all about, saying things like, "Is it a real diamond or some cheap fake?" and "Who would donate a cake with a diamond ring in it?"

Trixi announced in a voice loud enough for everyone to hear, "According to the *Extra Special Edition of the Upland Green Gossiper,* it's a genuine diamond. Plus, there might be more diamonds hidden in other cakes!"

A stampede of adults and kids crashed through the doors of the Cake Walk room, clamoring to buy tickets. Poor Mrs. Bryson was racing back and forth, trying to sell tickets while keeping people from poking and prodding the prize cakes.

"Mission accomplished in the Cake Walk," Trixi said. "I wonder what'll happen next?"

"Let's go and find out," Martin said, heading for the gym.

On their way, they ran into Ms. Baumgartner standing near the gym door.

"It's nice to see the Cake Walk doing so well, but the gym's completely empty," the principal said. "And I was just down at the auction and the Bingo room. Not a soul to be found."

"Oh, don't you worry, Ms. Baumgartner," Trixi said. "I think I hear something that's going to make you forget all your worries."

What Trixi heard was the roar of a gigantic tour bus pulling up to the front door of the school. In huge letters across the bus was *VIVA LAS VEGAS BINGO TOURS*. The door swung open, and a pack of Bingo players thundered out, holding their dabbers high.

"Third room on your right!" Trixi said. The crowd of blue-haired ladies raced down the hall and swarmed into the Bingo room. In minutes, it was standing room only, and every table was covered with Bingo cards. The bus driver staggered down the hall toward the Bingo room, his face covered in red and blue Bingo dabs.

"Are you okay?" Ms. Baumgartner said.

"We were on our way to Las Vegas on a Bingo tour when someone at the back of the bus said there was Bingo going on at the school. I told them it wasn't on the schedule, but they attacked me with their dabbers until I agreed to stop!"

"It looks like the Fall Fair Fundraiser might make a bit of money after all," Martin said.

"I have to admit, things are looking up," Ms. Baumgartner replied.

They were out of cakes at the Cake Walk, and the crowd was leaving the room grumbling about not finding any more diamonds. After all the excitement in the Cake Walk, there wasn't much interest in the games in the gym. All that changed when the front doors of the school swung open and in walked the town's mayor.

"Show me the Dunk Tank," Mayor Wainwright ordered.

"What's going on?" people asked as Mayor Wainwright strode down the hall to the gym. The town's mayor had never visited the school before, let alone come to the Fall Fair Fundraiser. As he walked through the doors of the gym, he threw off his long coat. Underneath, Mayor Wainwright was wearing his swimsuit and an Upland Green School T-shirt. He snapped his fingers, and Wally Lumkowski climbed out of the Dunk Tank. The mayor took his place on the seat high above the water.

As word of the mayor's arrival spread, dozens of people streamed into the gym. Shocked to see their mayor sitting in the Dunk Tank, no one knew what to do. Would it be proper to try to dunk him? Everyone stood around, waiting, watching.

Then Mayor Wainwright shouted, "Hey, you! Mr. Brent Parker! The way you throw a baseball, you couldn't hit the broad side of a barn! You couldn't dunk me if you bought a million-dollars worth of tickets!"

"Oh yeah?" Mr. Parker replied. "Just watch me!" He bought a handful of tickets, stepped up and took aim at the Dunk Tank target, launching ball after ball. It turned out that Mayor Wainwright was right when he said Mr. Parker couldn't hit the broad side of a barn. After spending $27.50 on tickets, he finally hit the target, and Mayor Wainwright plummeted into the water with a great *SPLOOSH*!

The crowd cheered, and immediately a long lineup of adults formed, everyone wanting to take a crack at dunking the mayor. With each *whack* of the baseball against the target, and with each *sploosh* of the mayor in the Dunk Tank, the crowd cheered. Anyone who managed to dunk Mayor Wainwright became an instant hero.

While the adults were all having fun at the Dunk Tank, it wasn't half as much fun for the kids. "This is so boring. It's not fair," Tina Montgomery said to her friend, Alexis Smith. "The adults get to have all the fun while we just stand around here getting bored."

Trixi leaned toward Tina and whispered, "Hey, Tina. Why don't you go and try the Fish Pond. I'm sure you'll catch a great prize."

"You've obviously never tried the Fish Pond," Tina replied. "Do you have any idea how lame the prizes are? It's just for little kids."

But Tina's friend, Alexis, said, "Ah, why not? Anything's better than standing around being bored." Alexis headed over to the Fish Pond, bought a ticket and lowered her fishing line behind the cardboard. She felt a tug as her prize was hooked to the end of her line.

"I can't believe you're actually doing this," Tina said. "I outgrew the Fish Pond in grade one."

But as Alexis pulled her line out of the Fish Pond and saw what dangled on the end of her line, she let out a scream that caused all heads in the gym to turn her way.

"Is it…is it, like, for real?" Tina said.

"Yeah! It's for real!" Alexis said.

"Are you sure? It's probably some cheapo-plastic thing that doesn't even work," Tina said.

"No, it's not! It's for real! My uncle's got a watch just like this, only this one's solid gold!"

Word travelled quickly throughout the gym that the Fish Pond wasn't your average cardboard fishing hole. A huge lineup suddenly formed, stretching across the gym. No one figured they were too old for the Fish Pond when solid gold watches were swimming around in it.

Between the Dunk Tank and the Fish Pond, the gym was one great big moneymaker for the Fall Fair Fundraiser. Trixi and Martin had never seen Ms. Baumgartner smile so wide.

Amid the moneymaking mayhem in the gym, Martin managed to get the principal's attention. "Excuse me, Ms. Baumgartner, but how do you think the auction's going?"

"Terribly," Ms. Baumgartner replied, still grinning. "But who cares? Everyone's here in the gym spending their life savings trying to dunk the mayor or catch a gold watch! There's no one left to bid at the auction!"

"Maybe we should check it out, just in case," Martin said. "I read somewhere that a special visitor would be coming to the auction."

"Oh, really? Who?" Ms. Baumgartner said. But Martin was already leading her down the hall toward the front door. Through the glass doors, they could see the outline of a car—a very, very long, dark, shiny stretch limo—pulling right up to the door. Two muscle-bound men wearing black suits and dark glasses jumped out, glanced around suspiciously and then opened one of the rear doors.

Out of the back of the limousine stepped a tall slim man in a golf shirt, plaid pants and white shoes. Handing a briefcase to one of his bodyguards, he breezed through the front door of the school and headed straight for the music room.

Ms. Baumgartner's jaw dropped. "Is that who I think it is?"

"It sure is, Ms. Baumgartner," Martin said. "None other than multi-gajillionaire Howie 'The Hound' Barker! Take three guesses what's in that briefcase, and the first two guesses don't count!"

Ms. Baumgartner didn't need to take a guess. She scrambled down to the music room, arriving just in time to hear the auctioneer say, "We have item number seven, a pair of hand-knit slippers, made with loving and tender care by Mrs. Olive Broom. We'll start the bidding at two dollars. Do I hear two dollars? Two dollars for these beautiful, one-of-a-kind slippers!"

"Five thousand dollars!" called a voice from the back of the room.

The auctioneer chuckled and said, "Sorry, sir. For a minute, I thought you said five thousand dollars."

"That's exactly what I said. Five thousand dollars!"

"Listen, sir. I've got an auction to run here. I don't have time for jokers like you!" the auctioneer said.

"I bid five thousand dollars!" Howie Barker shouted.

"Okay, then." The auctioneer banged his gavel, and said, "Sold! To the man who owes the school five thousand dollars!"

A bodyguard brought the briefcase to the front of the room, popped it open and handed the auctioneer five thick bundles of cash.

"That's...that's...like...real money!" the auctioneer said. He handed over the pink knitted slippers, which the bodyguard placed carefully in the briefcase. He snapped it shut and headed to the back of the room.

The auctioneer, who made his living with fast talking, was left speechless.

"Excuse me, but I think we'd better get on with the auction!" Martin said.

"Right! The auction!" the auctioneer said, still shaking his head in disbelief. "Okay, then. Item number eight. A pair of hand-carved chopsticks made by Byron Williams. We'll start the bidding at..."

"Eight thousand dollars!" Martin shouted.

"Are you kidding me, kid? You actually have—?"

"Ten thousand!" Howie Barker shouted.

The auctioneer's head jerked back and forth from Martin to Howie Barker and back to Martin again. "Are you crazy? Are you *loco*? Ten thousand dollars for a pair of lousy hand-carved chopsticks! You must be out of your mind!"

"Twelve thousand!" Howie Barker shouted.

Martin jumped up on the platform, took the gavel from the auctioneer, banged it on the podium and said, "Sold to the man with the matching bodyguards!" Once again, one of the bodyguards hustled to the front of the room and handed over twelve stacks of bills, while the auctioneer handed over the spindly wooden chopsticks.

Without another word, Howier Barker and his two bodyguards breezed out the back door of the music room to their awaiting limo.

"Not a bad price for some slippers and a pair of chopsticks," Martin said to Ms. Baumgartner. "I hate to think of what he would have paid for the pizza."

☆ ☆ ☆

At 9:00 PM, Trixi and Martin stood outside the office and watched the waterlogged mayor slosh his way down the hall, headed for home. Their dabbers all dry, the Bingo players scuttled out of the school and back onto their bus. The fishing rods were put away for another year, and the last few remaining people trudged home without a penny left in their pockets. The last person out of the gym was Mrs. Green, staggering under the weight of a bulging garbage bag full of money.

"Do you need a hand with that, Mrs. Green?" Martin said.

"That would be wonderful, Martin. Usually, I can carry the money we make from the games in the gym in a small grocery bag. But not this year."

Trixi and Martin each grabbed one side of the garbage bag and shuffled down the hall toward the office. Mrs. Bryson was lugging an enormous bag of money from the Cake Walk, while Mr. Quigley was dragging a bag with each hand down the hall from the Bingo room.

Ms. Baumgartner stood at the office door, clapping. "You can just leave it on the floor for now," she said. "First I have to clean off my desk, and then we can count it there."

☆ ☆ ☆

Outside the school, Trixi couldn't contain herself.

"That was great! No, it wasn't! It was more than great! It was terrific! No, it wasn't! It was more than terrific! It was fantastic! No, it wasn't! It was more than fantastic!" she shouted, pirouetting along the sidewalk. "It was…it was… an A-plus, A-okay, super-colossal, mega-gnarly, not-half-bad, like-wow, peacherina, knock-out, rip-snortin', hunky-dory, killer-diller, bees-knees HUUUUMDINGER!"

But Martin trudged along the walkway like he was wearing lead underwear.

"I agree that the Fall Fair Fundraiser was a success," he said. "And I suppose we achieved what we set out to accomplish, but…"

"But what?" Trixi said. She grabbed Martin by the chin and pulled his head up so they were eye to eye. "Can't you get it through that goopy gunky brain of yours that we are now heroes? Everything happened tonight because of us! We did it!

Before she went to Photocopy Heaven, Gwennie came through for us big time!"

"Yeah, but…"

"Yeah, but WHAT?" Trixi said.

"Maybe *you* know we're heroes, and *I* know we're heroes, but does Ms. Baumgartner know we're heroes? If she still thinks you're a troublemaking pain and my newspaper is a doomed money-loser, it doesn't matter what we think. You'll still be washing school buses on Saturday mornings, and I still won't have my newspaper back."

"Don't you worry your little head, Marty!" Trixi said. "It's mission accomplished!"

Martin wasn't so sure.

SEVENTEEN

At school the next morning, Martin arrived early and headed straight for his locker. In spite of last night's wild Fall Fair Fundraiser, everything looked normal. There was no evidence of stampeding Bingo players, pulverized cakes or water-logged mayors, and the stacks of money had been safely stashed away in the school's safe. When the bell rang for the start of the day, everything seemed perfectly ho-hum.

Moments after Martin settled into his seat in class, Ms. Baumgartner came on the PA. Her voice sounded louder and more harsh than normal. "Trixi Wilder and Martin Wettmore! To my office. Immediately!"

This didn't sound good. Martin slumped over in his desk, his forehead resting on his math book. Now what? he thought. Maybe she found out about the extra special edition of the newspaper. Maybe she didn't care that it helped the school raise thousands of dollars for the library. Maybe Ms. Baumgartner was being her usual unfair self.

"Martin!" his teacher said. "You heard the announcement. Down to the office. Immediately!"

When Trixi heard the announcement, she walked to the nearest wall and thumped her forehead three times. Then, she looked toward the ceiling and shouted, "I don't believe it! I really don't believe it! I knew I never should have listened to that Martin Wettmore! Doing good never pays!"

"Trixi!" her teacher said. "You heard the announcement. Down to the office. Immediately!"

Trixi and Martin arrived at the principal's office at the same time and sat in their usual small, yellow, plastic chairs. Trixi looked at the ceiling, while Martin looked at the floor. Ms. Baumgartner was out in the office talking to Mrs. Sledge.

"She's probably keeping us waiting on purpose just to torture us," Trixi whispered.

"Mr. Pen phoned today," Mrs. Sledge was saying. "He has a new job, so he'll be unable to service our new photocopier."

"Maybe she found out about our late night visit to the photocopy room, and now she'll blame us for destroying the photocopier," Martin whispered.

"A new job?" Ms. Baumgartner said. "Wherever did Mr. Pen get a new job?"

"He told me he was going to be repairing photocopiers at the offices of the Science Fiction Writers of Canada."

The principal whirled about and marched into her office. She was all business, handing Martin and Trixi each a sheet of paper, then walking behind her desk and sitting down.

"Ms. Baumgartner! I can explain everything!" Martin said. "We were only trying to help! Honest!"

"It was all Martin's idea!" Trixi said.

"It wasn't just me!" Martin said. "You helped!"

"Forget it! It was your idea all along!" Trixi stood up, and Martin stood to face her.

"You're nothing but a big pain, Trixi!"

"Oh yeah? What about you? You are the most…"

"ENOUGH! SIT! BOTH OF YOU!" Ms. Baumgartner said. "I don't want to hear any more arguing. As far as I'm concerned, you're both equally responsible."

There was a long, awkward silence, with Ms. Baumgartner's eyes flitting back and forth between the two of them. "Well? Aren't you going to read what I've given you?" she said finally.

They looked down at the sheets of paper Ms. Baumgartner had handed them. Across the top were the words, the *All New Upland Green Examiner.* In the top corner was today's date. Below that was a great big headline:

FALL FAIR FUNDRAISER RAKES IN RECORD AMOUNT OF CASH!
TWO STUDENTS BECOME INSTANT HEROES!

✩ ✩ ✩

On Wednesday night at 8:58 PM, Trixi Wilder was sprawled across the plush pink carpet next to her pink canopy bed. The TV was off, along with her cell phone, satellite radio, CD, DVD and Mp3 players. Trixi wanted no distractions, for she was writing the best story she had ever written in her entire life.

"Yes! You've definitely outdone yourself this time," she whispered. "This is definitely the best one yet!" Trixi sprang up off the floor and ran across the room to her computer. She typed in the story, checked it once, checked it twice, then checked it once more, just in case, before e-mailing it away. Seconds after she'd clicked Send, she ran to her bedside table, picked up her cell phone and hit the top name on her speed-dial list.

"Hey, Marty! I sent you the story I did on the juggling club...You got it already? Wow! That was quick. So? How's it look?" Trixi grabbed a pen and pad of paper and held the phone between her shoulder and her cheek.

"Oh, yeah. I always get *R-E-A-D* and *R-E-E-D* mixed up... Yeah, I guess the spell-checker wouldn't pick that up. What else?...Those darn apostrophes! So it comes before the *s* with *people's*. I think I get it. Okay, what else?...That's it? Are you sure? You mean I even spelled *discombobulation* right? I don't think my spell-checker had ever heard of the word, so I just kind of sounded it out. That's amazing. Thanks. Talk to you later."

☆ ☆ ☆

On Wednesday night at 9:37 PM, Martin Wettmore rubbed his eyes. Except for a few phone calls, he'd been staring at his computer screen pretty well nonstop since three thirty that afternoon. Beside Martin's keyboard was a stack of thirty pages, each covered in his neat precise handwriting. On the bulletin board above his desk was a pile of fifteen photographs printed off a digital camera.

The door to his room flew open, and Razor barged in, lugging his electric guitar and amp.

"Razor! It's Wednesday night. My night to work on the paper. Remember?" Martin said.

"Is it Wednesday already?" Razor said, picking up his guitar and amp. "You got any aliens in your paper this week?"

"Not so far, but you never know," Martin said.

"Hope so. You can never go wrong with aliens," Razor said as he climbed out the window onto the garage roof.

"Martin!" It was his mother. "One of Sissy's dogs just pooped in the hall! It's your turn to clean it up!"

"Remember what we agreed? They're Sissy's dogs, so if they poop in the hall, she has to clean it up."

"But she's baking dog treats," his mother said.

"It's Wednesday night. It's my newspaper night. Remember? We talked about this."

"Right," his mother said.

"And Mom?"

"What is it, Martin?"

"After the article on your pickles last week, everyone's asking me for your recipe."

"Sorry, Martin. It's a family secret. But you can have one of Sissy's dog-treat recipes if you want."

"I'll think about it," Martin said. "And there's something else, Mom," Martin said. "Internet's down. I'm trying to send an e-mail and I'm not connecting."

"I forgot to tell you. Blinky got hold of the modem and chewed it to pieces."

Martin closed his eyes and sighed. Picking up his stack of papers, he carefully walked down the stairs to the phone in the kitchen and dialed a number from memory.

"Hi, Trixi. It's me. One of Sissy's dogs chewed our modem, and I've got a couple of things I want to clear up. I interviewed the music teacher today, and I'm working on the article. Do you think I should mention her punk-rock band first, or should I talk about her time as the lead bagpipe player in a country and western band?…Yeah, it makes sense. I'll play up the punk-rock thing, for sure…And I'm working on that story about the missing garbage cans. It seems really dull, so I'm looking for a different angle. Any suggestions?…Yeah, alien theft sounds good, but only if I say it's your theory. We have to make that clear…That's good too. I'll check with Ms. Baumgartner to see if she'll put up a reward…Yeah, I'll drop my part off at your place on my way to school. It's your turn to copy it, right?…Sounds good. Talk to you later."

✩ ✩ ✩

At 9:23 PM, Trixi tiptoed downstairs to her father's office. The door was closed, so she slipped a piece of paper under his door and then moved down the hall. Her mother's door was also closed, so she did the same. By the time she'd returned to her room, there were two e-mail messages waiting for her.

The first one read: *I am so proud of you, Trixi. In just the last few weeks, your spelling and grammar has improved immeasurably. I knew our talk with your principal would straighten things out. Love, Mom.*

The second one said: *You never told me Mrs. Primrose was a guest writer for your paper. Her recipe for Black Forest cake looks mouthwatering. I wish she'd bake us one when we're around. Love, Dad.*

✩ ✩ ✩

At 10:22 PM, Razor was standing beside Martin's printer as it hummed and buzzed and spat out two sheets. Razor snatched them up and glanced at a mouse running across the top of the printer with a pickle in its mouth. As the last sheet left the printer, the lights went out, Martin's computer shut down and the printer died.

"Mom must have plugged the toaster in again," Razor said. "You got a flashlight I can use?"

"Remember. It's still not the final version, but it's close," Martin said. "You'll be happy to know that I managed to work in an alien again this week."

☆ ☆ ☆

The next morning, Trixi arrived at school extra early. She used a key the principal had given her to open the door to the photocopy room, punched her four-digit access code into the new photocopier and got to work.

☆ ☆ ☆

Just before recess, Martin set up a table outside the office and put a large metal box with a hole in the top on the table. A minute later, Trixi arrived with a stack of newspapers.

"I made twenty extra copies after what happened last week," she said.

"Good thinking," Martin replied.

When the recess bell sounded, Martin held up a copy of this week's edition of the *Upland Green Examiner* and shouted, "Get your paper here! Read all about it! An interview with our very own music teacher, Mrs. Cargill!"

Trixi added, "Was she really the lead guitarist in a punk-rock band called The Grooveyard? Read this week's paper for all the details!"

"Read all about it!" Martin called out. "*Garbage Cans Mysteriously Disappear!*"

Then Trixi said, "Was it the work of aliens? Read about how you can earn a big reward for their return—the garbage cans, not the aliens!"

"Read all about it!"

And, of course, everyone at Upland Green School did.

ACKNOWLEDGMENTS

FUTURE AUTHOR'S PARENTS ALLOW CHILD'S
IMAGINATION TO RUN OFF-LEASH!

HIGHLAND PARK ELEMENTARY STAFF
AND STUDENTS INSPIRE AUTHOR
TO WRITE NOVEL WITH HELP OF AN
ALTER-EGO SWINE!

EDITOR SARAH HARVEY WIELDS
MAGICAL BLUE PENCIL!

GOVERNMENT OFFICIALS ACKNOWLEDGE
THAT TEACHER-LIBRARIANS REALLY DO
RULE THE WORLD!